Kirsty expected the old familiar thrill

And yet Simon's arrival at her party left her somehow empty. He was very handsome, the same old Simon, but now she could not stir up any response, even when he kissed her.

Later, standing a little apart from the rest of the party, she glanced from Simon to Gyles, who was busy in conversation. Gyles's face in profile seemed hard and autocratic until she remembered the warmth in his eyes when he had smiled at her earlier that evening. Slowly she looked again from one to the other of the two men, both unaware of her scrutiny.

It seemed a very strange time and place to discover that she had got over an infatuation for one man only to fall headlong in love with another!

Garden of Thorns

by

SALLY WENTWORTH

Harlequin Books

TORONTO • LONDON • LOS ANGELES • AMSTERDAM
SYDNEY • HAMBURG • PARIS • STOCKHOLM • ATHENS • TOKYO

Original hardcover edition published in 1980
by Mills & Boon Limited

ISBN 0-373-02361-8

Harlequin edition published October 1980

CHAPTER ONE

THE door of Briar Cottage was standing wide open, and Kirsty's heart sank as she went inside and saw that there were already a lot of people gathered there, some still looking round the house, others standing about waiting for the auction to start. Briefly she considered going over the place again, but then rejected the idea; she had looked over it thoroughly on her earlier visit a week ago and knew the details in the prospectus almost off by heart, so carefully had she studied them. From the hall she crossed to the sitting-room, remembering that the levels were different and that you had to step down into the room. Two men were examining the dirty, soot-stained tiles of the fireplace, but Kirsty went past them to the latticed window and sat on the deep window-seat to look out at the garden. There was little to see, of course, just a tangled, overgrown expanse of weeds and grass beneath the gnarled old fruit trees, their leafless branches bent and swaying before the icy February wind. It looked completely dreary and dismal.

Kirsty shivered as the wind found its way through the broken window-panes, and she turned back into the room. This, too, was in a terribly neglected state; plaster flaked from the walls and in the far corner a damp patch had discoloured the ceiling, although most of it was concealed by hanging cobwebs. The woodwork, as in the rest of the cottage, was painted a muddy chocolate colour, and she guessed that the previous owner must have got hold of a job lot of paint

5

and just slapped it on. It all looked terribly depressing, and for a moment she wondered what on earth she was doing here; she must be mad to even contemplate realising their capital, which had been so carefully invested, and spending it all on this decrepit old place. It would take so much work to get it decent, be a total time- and energy-consuming task.

She gave herself a little shake; that was what she wanted, wasn't it? The whole idea of buying a house with some land that could be made productive was that she could get Penny away from London and give her something to work at and look forward to. And she was desperate to find somewhere. She had been looking for nearly three weeks before she found Briar Cottage, and although it was in a far worse condition than she had been looking for, she had enough imagination to see that once the place had been put in order, the cottage, with its low-hanging thatched roof, could be a delightful house to live in, and, most important of all, the three acres of garden would provide them with a livelihood.

But by far the most urgent problem was to get Penny away from the ruinous influence of the crowd she had got mixed up with recently. Kirsty still shuddered at the memory of having to sit in a court and hear the magistrates try her sister. Only just nineteen, and younger than Kirsty by nearly three years, Penny had got involved with a youth she had met soon after leaving school and had been completely besotted by him. It was obvious from the young man's moody, sullen character that the relationship would lead to nothing but disaster, and Kirsty had done her best to persuade Penny to give him up, but this had only led to rows until Penny had walked out of their apartment without saying where she was going. She was over eighteen, there wasn't a thing Kirsty could do about it, and she hadn't seen Penny again until the police had called a month ago in the early hours of the morning to say that the youth had been caught while burgling a house and that Penny had been waiting for him in the getaway car and had also been arrested. Frantic with worry, Kirsty had gone to bail her sister out and had found her frightened and extremely chastened. The younger girl had sworn that she hadn't known her boyfriend was committing a crime; he'd merely told her to wait while he visited a friend, and Kirsty had believed her. Fortunately the magistrates had too, but only after probationary reports, and they'd given her a solemn warning about her future conduct that had made a distinct impression.

A great many things had come to light at the trial, among them that the man had been in prison before and also that he was already married. That had really hurt Penny, who'd been convinced they would eventually get married, and ever since she had been in a state of deep depression, shutting herself away and often having bouts of prolonged weeping.

After the hearing the police Inspector had taken Kirsty aside and advised her to get Penny right away. 'We can't prove it,' he told her, 'but there's a strong possibility your sister's boy-friend is passing drugs. Get her as far away from him as possible, because he's bound to come looking for her when he gets out of prison. And find her something else to think about, something that will keep her completely occupied.'

There was some bustle in the doorway and Kirsty saw that people were moving out into the hall. She followed the two men who had been looking at the fireplace and heard one mutter something about, 'The wall's plenty thick enough for an inglenook', before

she gave her attention to the auctioneer. He was standing on the stairs to get a better view, but as there were
so many people some had to go and stand on the upstairs landing. From her position at the back Kirsty
looked at the people, wondering how many of them
were serious prospective buyers. There was a young
couple with excited faces, the girl with a brightly new
wedding ring on her finger, who pushed eagerly to the
front, and near the auctioneer at the foot of the stairs
there was a youngish man in an expensive-looking
camel overcoat who carried a documents case under his
arm. But there was no time to look further because the
auctioneer had started to speak, giving details of the
size and age of the property.

The first few bids came tentatively. Ten thousand
pounds. Twelve thousand from the young couple.
Then they came more quickly as a man who looked
like a farmer joined in to raise it to fifteen before someone on the landing out of her sight raised it again. The
young couple dropped out, their faces crestfallen,
while the farmer and the unknown bidder fought it
out to twenty thousand. This was too much for the
farmer, who gave a shrug of defeat. The portly auctioneer asked for any other bids and lifted his hammer,
thinking it was all over. Kirsty raised her voice for the
first time.

'Twenty-one thousand,' she said firmly.

There was a murmur among the onlookers and they
turned to peer over their shoulders at the tall, slim
girl whose shoulder-length fair hair framed an attractive face with clear, pale-violet eyes and well-shaped
mouth.

'Twenty-one and a half.' The unseen male voice
from the landing again.

'Twenty-two.'

The price went up by five hundred pounds at a time to twenty-six thousand, the man sounding angrier by each bid, until he dropped out. Kirsty looked at the auctioneer expectantly, her face flushed, her pulses racing with excitement. But then there was a movement near the stairs as the well-dressed man raised his hand to attract attention.

'Twenty-seven,' he said decisively.

Kirsty groaned inwardly; she had been so certain it was hers, and at a reasonable price too. 'Twenty-eight,' she said clearly, hoping that the new bidder would be put off.

But he refused to be intimidated and took the price up to thirty-one thousand before he showed any sign of hesitation. Kirsty dug her nails into her palms. Her limit had been thirty thousand; she would need the rest of their capital to repair the house and clear the garden. If she went any higher it would leave them very short. But gardening was the one thing that Penny had ever really loved, and it had been the only scheme that had roused her from her misery and apathy and for which she had shown the slightest enthusiasm. I've got to have this place, Kirsty thought desperately, it might take me months to find another. 'Thirty-two,' she said defiantly, wiping away the smile that had started to show on the other bidder's face.

He seemed to wrestle with himself, then said, albeit reluctantly, 'Thirty-three.'

The crowd looked at Kirsty expectantly. 'Thirty-four,' she called out recklessly.

The man glared at her angrily, then shook his head at the auctioneer. The hammer came down at last. Briar Cottage was hers! Kirsty felt a wave of dizzy relief and had to lean back against the flaking wall for support. The other people glanced at her curiously as they began to depart, some of those who had hoped to buy the cottage giving her dirty looks as they passed, but Kirsty was blind to all of them.

Coming down the stairs, the auctioneer crossed to her and said grimly, 'I trust you are able to meet your bid, young lady?'

Anger flicked her at his patronising tone and she straightened up. 'Certainly,' she replied coldly. 'I have a covering letter from my bank to verify that I have the amount required in my account. I'll give you a cheque for the ten per cent deposit now and pay the balance just as soon as the exchange of contracts can be completed.'

He took the letter from her and read it through.

'How soon do you think I'll be able to move in?' Kirsty asked him anxiously.

'As you're paying cash it's merely a matter of paperwork. Three weeks at the most, I should think.' He looked at her in open curiosity. 'But surely you intend to have the cottage repaired and decorated before you move in, Miss Naylor? I can give you the names of some local firms who are very reliable.' He fished in his pocket and held out two or three trade cards.

'Thank you,' Kirsty said firmly, 'but I doubt if I shall be needing those. We intend to do all the work ourselves.'

'Oh, I see.' The man's brow cleared. 'You're about to be married. Well, tell your fiancé to get in touch with us and we'll get things moving straight away.'

Kirsty glared at the auctioneer, annoyed by his pompous assumption that she was incapable of acting for herself. 'No, I'm not getting married,' she snapped at him, her violet eyes frosty. 'I'm buying this place myself, and *I'm* telling you *now* to start work on the transaction at once. Here's the name and address of my lawyers; I want this to go through as promptly as possible, you understand?'

The poor man looked completely taken aback, but recovered quickly; after all, she was a buyer and was indirectly paying his fees. 'I beg your pardon, Miss Naylor. Our firm will, of course, do everything in its power to make the transfer as quick and as smooth as possible.'

He motioned her to precede him out of the hall and Kirsty watched as he locked the heavy wooden front door. Looking up, she stared at the dirty dormer windows, almost hidden beneath the ragged thatch and the thick stems of a climbing rose. Vaguely she wondered what colour it was, and then felt the first thrill of ownership as she realised that in a few months' time she would be here, living in the cottage, and would find out for herself.

She turned to walk down the narrow path ahead of the auctioneer. At the gate she stopped and said, 'That man who bid against me at the end—the one carrying a briefcase. Who was he?'

'Oh, that was a junior in the firm of lawyers who act for the Squire.'

'The Squire?'

'Gyles Grantham. He owns all the land hereabouts. His house is further along that lane that goes down the side of your property. It's called Notley Manor.'

He shook her hand and walked towards his big maroon Jaguar. Kirsty went the other way to her small yellow Mini. But she didn't drive off immediately, instead she sat and gazed unseeingly through the windscreen. She'd done it! She'd really done it! Now she and Penny were the owners of a tumbledown cottage and a piece of land that they hoped to turn into a pro-

ductive garden where they would cultivate herbs to
sell commercially. It wasn't a decision they had taken
lightly, they had talked round and round it for hours
and studied books from the library to try and find out
whether it would be a viable proposition. But you can
only learn so much from books, and the only way they
would ever really know would be by finding out for
themselves. And Penny had been so keen, she had
really got above her depression and once more looked
like the girl she used to be. And that was worth giving up a lot for. Because buying Briar Cottage meant
that Kirsty would have to sacrifice a lot: her comfortable modern apartment in Swiss Cottage, the job she
loved as a librarian in a well-known teaching hospital,
and most of all her blossoming friendship with Simon
Granger, whom she'd met when he came to the hospital as a surgeon working for his Fellowship.

Kirsty sighed a little, but then tried to shake off the
momentary feeling of depression. If they were going to
make this enterprise succeed, they would need all her
drive and enthusiasm, there could be no half measures,
no wishful looking back at what might have been.
And besides, if Simon cared enough they would find
a way to keep on seeing each other no matter how
much distance separated them.

Right now her biggest worry was going to be finding enough capital to get them started. By spending
four thousand over their limit they would have nothing to fall back on to cover any unforeseen difficulties.
The money was from the estate left equally between
them on the death of their parents many years ago. It
had been carefully invested for them by their grand-
parents, who had brought them up and had paid for
a good education, but now that they were of age Kirsty
felt justified in using the money in this way. She

frowned rather worriedly for a moment but then straightened her shoulders, her chin defiant. Well, right or wrong, she had burned her boats and there was no going back now.

Starting the car, she drove slowly along the road. Briar Cottage was almost at the edge of the village of Notley, and she passed several other cottages before the road widened and she came to a large village green. On the left was the ancient village church, half hidden by trees, its stone tower topped by a spire, and it was hardly necessary to look at the weathrcock on the top to know that this freezing cold wind was coming from the north. The wind had kept the villagers indoors and there were no customers for the post office-cum-general store or the greengrocers further along, although there were several cars in the car-park of the whitewashed pub with its higgledy-piggledy roofline denoting later additions to the original building. Its sign creaked and groaned in the strong wind and Kirsty could just make it out: The Mops and Brooms. What an odd name! There were a few largish Georgian-style houses on the other side of the green, then a row of terraced cottages, a garage, and a small estate of modern houses that seemed completely out of place before she was through the village and heading for the main road to London, eager to get to the apartment and tell Penny all about their new home.

The next few weeks were the most hectic that Kirsty had ever known. She gave in her notice from her job straight away, and luckily her employers were most considerate and allowed her to have time off to visit her lawyer and her bank to make all the financial arrangements. Her Mini she traded in for a much more practical van, and then she had to arrange to give up her apartment and start packing all their possessions.

'Whew, I never realised that moving was such a load of work,' she remarked to Simon when they managed to meet for a quick coffee in the staff canteen one afternoon. 'I spent the whole of my lunch hour today queueing up at the post office and filling in forms to notify them of my change of address.'

'Have you got a moving date yet?'

'Yes, the first of March. That's next Thursday. Now all I've got to do is to find a removal firm who aren't booked up for that day, although it's very short notice,' she added rather worriedly.

'Look, why don't you leave it until the Saturday? I've got that weekend free and I'll get hold of a large van so that we can do the move ourselves. Rory and Philip are free too,' he added, mentioning two of his fellow surgeons. 'I'm sure they'd be pleased to give us a hand. Tell you what, we could bring our sleeping-bags with us and stay overnight, perhaps make a start on the garden for you on Sunday.'

'Oh, Simon, could you? That would be lovely. I've been dreading the actual move.' She looked at him gratefully.

He reached out to cover her hand, his hazel eyes under his mop of longish brown hair smiling into hers. 'For you—anything.'

Kirsty turned her hand so that she could hold tightly to his. She liked him so much; he was always gentle and kind and great fun to be with, seldom serious, although he was reputed in the hospital to be an extremely good doctor with a great future in surgery. Not that you'd ever think it to look at him, she thought with a little smile, for he hated wearing a suit and was far happier in sweater and jeans, but then so were most of the young doctors and medical students at the hospital; now only the more senior members of the staff appeared in business suits every day.

In the end their moving day turned almost into a party. Another recently married doctor had come to help and had brought along his wife, which made seven of them. Kirsty had everything packed ready in tea-chests and boxes when they arrived very early on the Saturday morning with the van. And what a van! Simon had borrowed one belonging to the hospital band, which they used to transport themselves and their instruments. It was bright blue and had, 'If music be the food of love, play on', emblazoned on the sides in huge yellow letters. Added to which some amateur artist had lovingly painted flowers and trees in every available space. Kirsty burst out laughing when she saw it and then the men proceeded to get in each other's way as they loaded the furniture with a great deal of joking and rude comments, until Penny said rather tartly, 'I hope they're better doctors than they are removal men!'

At last they were ready and Kirsty hurried to lead the way in her own van with no time for a last look around the apartment, no time to take leave of her old life before she began the new. But perhaps it was better this way. She glanced at Simon sitting next to her with Penny squeezed in beside him on the other side. And perhaps he had intended it to be like this; he, more than anyone, knew just how sad she was to leave.

They stopped for a belated breakfast on the way, so it was almost noon before Kirsty pulled up outside Briar Cottage. She looked at Penny anxiously, wondering what her sister would think of her choice. 'Well, this is it,' she said over-heartily.

Penny got out of the van and walked to the gate, looking up at the cottage much as Kirsty had done the day she bought it. In looks the sisters were very similar, both having fair hair, but Penny was shorter and her face lacked the fineness of feature of Kirsty's, so that Penny was only pretty whereas Kirsty was almost beautiful. For a long moment she stared at the house and then she turned to them.

Her face split into a big grin. 'It's great!' she enthused. 'I just can't wait to get started on it!'

Kirsty felt a great surge of relief; she had been so afraid that Penny might have taken a dislike to the place on sight. She found that she had been gripping Simon's hand hard and now he put his arm round her and gave her a hug.

'Come on, open up. Let's see what the place is like inside.'

They walked up the garden path, followed by the others who were dressed in a motley collection of colourful sweaters, scarves, jeans, boots, all their old casual clothes for their working weekend. Rather tremblingly Kirsty inserted the key and went to push the door open.

'Wait!' Rory exclaimed. 'This is a great moment, we have to do it properly.' He ran back to the van and came back with a bottle of sparkling wine. 'Here you are, launch it with this.'

Laughingly Kirsty took the bottle from him and made Penny hold it with her while they smashed the neck against the wall of the cottage. Rory had given it a good shake so it made a terrific bang and they all cheered noisily. He then produced some paper cups filched from the coffee machine at the hospital and they all drank a toast. 'To Briar Cottage. May God bless her and all who sail in her,' Rory intoned with complete lack of imagination.

They all cheered again and then Simon stooped to put Kirsty over his shoulder in a very unromantic fireman's lift. 'I insist on carrying you over the threshold,' he announced.

Kirsty shrieked as he picked her up and grabbed hold of him, still clutching the bottle in her other hand. 'You fool, you'll drop me!'

'Are you denigrating my manhood?' he demanded in mock anger, and ran down the path with her just to show her how strong he was.

She yelled in pretended fright, then glanced up to find herself looking straight at a man who had got out of a white Range-Rover parked on the other side of the road and had been staring at the painted hospital van in amazement, but as she yelled he turned round and looked at her, still hanging over Simon's shoulder and waving the bottle. She got the impression that he was tall, dark, and broad-shouldered, but it was his face that made her go suddenly silent, for his eyes, hard as grey steel, were regarding her with a look of furious anger. For a moment he continued to glare at her, but his expression changed to one of disgust as his eyes ran over them all, then he turned abruptly, got back into his car and drove away down the lane at the side of the cottage.

The visual impact of those few seconds left Kirsty feeling distinctly shaken and she was rather subdued as Simon finally carried her through the front door and set her down in the hall. They insisted that she conduct them round herself and she tried to join naturally in their merriment as they explored the big kitchen on the left of the hall with its ancient range, the sitting-room on the other side, and then the two corresponding bedrooms upstairs and the Victorian-looking bathroom squeezed in between. But somehow she couldn't shake off the feeling of dismay the unknown man had given her. Why had he looked so angry? Admittedly they had been making rather a noise, but surely that wasn't sufficient reason for the almost murderous glare he'd given her. Kirsty frowned unhappily; the last thing she wanted to do was to antagonise their fellow-villagers, after all they would have to live alongside them, and she had a strong feeling that she and Penny would probably need all the help and advice they could get during the coming months when they would be striving to get their herb farm established. One of the others called out to her to unlock her van and she resolutely pushed her anxieties to the back of her mind. No good worrying about it now. Only time would show who the man was and whether his anger would have any effect on their lives in Briar Cottage.

By six o'clock that evening they were all exhausted, but at least they had removed all the surface grime and dirt from the two bedrooms, the bathroom and the kitchen so that they could bring in all the furniture. And by much searching around the men had found the stopcock in the garden so that they had running water, although the lights wouldn't come on because someone had carefully removed all the bulbs, and by the time they realised this it was already getting dark and all the village shops were shut.

'Where's the nearest town?' Simon asked. 'Barham, isn't it? What do you say we clean ourselves up and drive there for a meal? It's getting too dark to do anything more here.'

So they took turns to use the bathroom and drove into the town. They found a pleasant restaurant on the outskirts, but the manager took one look at their clothes and refused to let them in, so they ended up with hamburgers and chips in a Wimpy bar.

'This stuff's all right, but you never feel really full

up,' grumbled Rory, who devoted a great deal of time and thought to filling his stomach.

'Well, I did bring an electric cooker with me,' Kirsty pointed out. 'If we can plug that in we can cook our own food tomorrow.'

Simon laughed. 'Have you *looked* at the electric sockets in the cottage? They must have been installed when Edison first invented the stuff. The house needs complete rewiring or it will probably blow a fuse and set the whole place on fire.'

Kirsty looked at him in dismay. 'But that will cost a bomb—and we have to have something to cook on.'

'Why don't we get a couple of the hospital electricians to come down next weekend and do it for you as a spare-time job? That would cost you a lot less than if you got a contractor to do it—cut down on waiting time too.'

'Do you think they would?'

'Don't see why not. They don't get paid very much and would probably be glad of the opportunity to earn some extra cash.'

Penny had been listening to them quietly, but now she said eagerly, 'Why don't we use the range for cooking? Just like the other people who lived there did.'

'But, Penny, it's in a terrible state. I was going to throw it out.'

'Well, it could be cleaned, couldn't it? And it would give us some heat as well as providing an oven.'

'Yes, and I was looking at that fireplace in the sitting-room,' Rory put in. 'I'm sure it's a later addition and that there's an older fireplace behind it.'

Without thinking, Kirsty said, 'Yes, when I was buying the place I heard a man say he thought there was probably an inglenook in the wall.'

They picked this up immediately and before she

knew it the men had all decided they would remove
the tiled fireplace the following day to see what was
behind it.

'And I'll start cleaning the range,' Penny added enthusiastically.

Kirsty suddenly realised that her labour force, who
had come down with the definite objective of starting
work on the garden, had defected. She opened her
mouth to protest but saw the grins on their faces and
thought better of it. Rather a happy crowd doing
what they wanted than reluctant gardeners. When
they got back to the cottage it was too early to go to
bed, so they sat in a tight circle on the kitchen floor,
huddled together to keep warm, and told ghost stories
by the light of a torch. There was much moaning and
howling from the storytellers and Penny shrieked with
fright when Rory sneaked his hand behind her and
touched her neck at a particularly grisly point in his
story.

They went giggling to bed, men in one room, girls
in the other, and Kirsty insisted that Penny and the
other girl take the two single beds while she curled up
in a sleeping-bag. She slept at first, worn out by the
hard work of the day, but woke in the early hours,
frozen with cold. Shivering, she got up and pulled on
a dressing-gown over her nightdress. She remembered
that the spare blankets were still stacked in the hall, so
she pushed her feet into a pair of mules and slipped
quietly out of the room. The stairs creaked as she went
down, but the moon was shining brightly through the
uncurtained window on the half landing, and she had
no difficulty in finding a blanket. She was about to go
back up again, but gave a gasp of fear as she saw the
dark shape of someone standing on the stairs.

'It's all right, it's only me,' Simon's whispered voice assured her.

Kirsty leant against the wall in relief. 'Oh, you gave me such a scare! I thought you were a ghost.'

He came down and put his arm round her, pulling her down to sit beside him on the stairs. 'Can't you sleep?'

She shook her head. 'I was cold. This place is going to take some getting used to after a centrally heated apartment.'

'Here, I'll keep you warm.' Simon pulled her closer, his hands rubbing her arms, but presently his hands slowed as he drew her towards him and began to kiss her. At last he raised his head and said thickly, 'Oh, Kirsty, I'm going to miss you.' His hand cupped her breast over the thin cotton of her nightdress, his thumb gently caressing her. 'Life isn't going to be the same without your smile to look forward to every day after surgery.'

Gently Kirsty removed his hand and held it. 'You know I didn't want it this way. I had no choice. You must come down as often as you can.'

'I know.' He bent to kiss her again and then smiled as he said, 'But this place will really have a ghost soon; I'm going to haunt it regularly, you wait and see.'

They talked for a little longer, but then the cold drove them back to their sleeping-bags. Kirsty wrapped herself in the blanket and fell quickly asleep again, not waking until a hazy sunshine fell on her face. Getting up, she went to the window and looked out, realising that this was the first time she had been able to do so on a clear day. The garden was as tangled and overgrown as ever, but she looked past it to the unkempt hedge at the end of the garden, behind which lay a large field where a herd of Jersey cows were grazing. As she watched a man and a boy came to round them up and drive them through a gate towards a farm almost hidden in the fold of a hill. Then Kirsty caught her breath in a little gasp of pleasure. About a mile above the farm, on the flat piece of land on the brow of the hill and almost surrounded by trees, she could just make out a large E-shaped Tudor house of deep-red brickwork with tall, ornate chimneys. It looked so beautiful in the early morning sunlight, and so much part of the landscape, that it seemed to have grown there with the trees and to be destined to be there for ever. It was a lovely place, the kind you always dream about possessing.

She heard voices from the other bedroom and turned reluctantly, hurrying to get to the bathroom first, the more practical side of her nature taking over from the aesthetic.

Any hopes she had of making a start on the garden that day were doomed from the outset; as soon as she picked up a pair of secateurs and made a start on cutting back the rambler rose at the front of the cottage she was interrupted by demands for tools to take out the fireplace, metal polish to clean the brasswork on the range, where could they dump the rubbish, had she got a wire brush? Until in the end she just gave up and acted as general dogsbody, making coffee on the primus stove that Rory had brought with him, cutting sandwiches, and watching the kitchen get black with soot and dirt from the range and the sitting-room disappear beneath mounds of old bricks and concrete, while she expected the wall to collapse at any moment as the hole the men made got deeper and deeper.

But at four in the afternoon they triumphantly brought her into the room and showed her that they had been right. Exposed to the light of day again after goodness knows how many years was the huge oak beam supporting the chimney, and behind it the recess of the old fireplace, deep and high enough to walk right inside and wide enough to have roasted an animal carcase whole.

'Look,' Rory pointed. 'See that smaller hole at the back? That's what we think they used to use as the bread oven. The bricks around it held the heat and cooked the loaves slowly.'

'It's marvellous,' Kirsty applauded, trying not to think of how she was going to dispose of what looked like a couple of tons of rubble.

'Of course it still needs a lot of work doing to it,' Rory added. 'The brickwork needs rubbing down with a wire brush and the beam needs to be cleaned and treated, but we've done the biggest part of the job for you,' he said as if he'd done her a favour.

'Lord, look at the time!' Simon exclaimed. 'If we don't start back to London straight away we'll be like zombies in the morning, and I'm assisting at a brain op.'

They rushed round getting their things together and hastily threw them into the big van. Simon gave her a quick hug. 'Phone me during the week and I'll let you know about the electricians.' And then they were off, horn blaring, with Kirsty and Penny waving at the garden gate until they were out of sight. After they'd gone the two sisters looked at one another, feeling strangely bereft and alone.

'It was nice of them to come down, wasn't it?' Penny remarked. 'They were a great help.'

Kirsty walked into the house and looked at the shambles in the sitting-room. 'Oh, yes, they were a great help—but somehow I've a feeling that we would have got a lot more done if we'd been on our own.' And they both burst into rueful laughter.

The following morning they made a long list of things they needed and drove into the town to shop.

'I'm sure I noticed a garden centre a couple of miles

outside the town when we drove here the other night,'
Kirsty remarked. 'I'm hoping that we'll be able to
hire a rotovator, and perhaps a power saw to cut down
those dead trees. It would have been better if we could
have bought a rotovator, of course, but having to pay
more for the house puts that out of the question. We
shall need the rest of our capital to live on and to
buy plants to start us off.'

'There's the place,' Penny told her. Over on the
right.'

Kirsty pulled in to the car-park and they walked
towards the shop. It was very well laid out with a large
outdoor part displaying greenhouses, sheds and so on,
a huge hothouse full of indoor plants, and a
supermarket-type shop with bulbs, seeds, and everything else you could think of remotely connected with
gardening. As it was a Monday morning they had the
place to themselves, and when they told the assistant
what they wanted, they were directed to an office
where a rather dapper young man rose to greet them.

'Good morning. I'm the manager, Alan Morris.
What can I do for you ladies?' he said jocularly.

Kirsty explained what they wanted and arranged to
hire the tools straight away.

'I'll make out the forms, then. You realise you'll
have to pay a substantial deposit? It's expensive equip-
ment to have to replace if it gets damaged,' the manager told them.

'Yes, of course. I'll write you a cheque.' Kirsty
opened her bag and took out her cheque book, but
the manager shook his head regretfully.

'Sorry, but we insist on cash for deposits.'

'Oh, well, never mind. We've got to go into Barham
to do some shopping anyway. I'll go to the bank while
I'm there and we'll pick the tools up on the way back.'

'That will be fine. If you'll just fill in your name and address on the hire form.'

Kirsty did so and passed it back to him.

'Briar Cottage.' Alan Morris looked up and she thought she saw a flicker of recognition in his eyes, but it was gone so quickly that she might have been mistaken. 'Oh, yes, I heard that had been sold, but I didn't think anyone would have moved in so soon. Well, I'll see you later, then.' He came to open the door for them. 'It's always a pleasure to do business with two lovely young ladies like you,' he added fulsomely, running his eyes over them as they passed him, mentally undressing them.

'Yuk!' Penny said as soon as they got outside. 'I hope we don't have to deal with him too often. He made my flesh creep.'

'I know what you mean,' Kirsty agreed. 'He's the type who would take it as an invitation to start pawing you if you so much as smiled at him.'

They enjoyed exploring the old market town of Barham and had to make several trips back to the van as they made their purchases: a dozen light bulbs, a paraffin heater and fuel, food, a fork and handsaw—the list seemed endless. For lunch they had a basket snack in an old coaching inn, and discussed their plan of work beside a roaring fire.

'We must start on the garden,' Kirsty emphasised. 'After all, it's supposed to provide us with a living, and if we don't get it prepared now it will be too late to plant the herb seeds.'

'Not all of them have to be sown in March,' Penny pointed out. 'Tarragon, sage and chives should be planted in April. But I agree that the garden must be our first concern. What about the inglenook, though?'

'I'm just going to shut the door on that room and

forget it,' Kirsty replied firmly. 'Luckily the kitchen is plenty big enough to use as a living-room as well. We can put a couple of armchairs in there for the evenings and the rest of the furniture will have to stay in the bedrooms for the time being.' She looked at her watch. 'We'd better start getting back to the garden centre.'

They went straight into Alan Morris's office, expecting him to greet them as unctuously as he had before, but instead he seemed somewhat embarrassed.

'We've called to pick up the rotovator,' Kirsty reminded him.

'Er—yes.' He looked down at his desk, unwilling to meet their eyes. 'I'm afraid there's been a bit of a mix-up; we don't have the tools you want available, after all.'

'What? But you said this morning that——'

'I know I did, but as I said, the tools were already spoken for.' He shrugged. 'I'm sorry, but there it is.'

'Being sorry isn't good enough,' Kirsty retorted, her anger rising. 'You promised those tools to us. We had first claim.' She put her hands on the desk and leaned forward, glaring at the manager.

'It's no use getting angry with me, Miss Naylor. I'm only the manager here. I have to do as I'm told,' Alan Morris said defensively.

Kirsty gazed at him. 'Are you—are you trying to tell me that someone *told* you not to hire the tools out to us?'

He immediately looked discomfited. 'Well, I . . .' He ran a finger under his collar, his face unhappy. Then he seemed to make up his mind and leaned forward across the desk conspiratorially, his voice dropping. 'It was the owner. He came in after you'd gone and happened to see the form you filled in—it was still lying here on my desk. Then he just tore the form up and said that he would be needing all the rotovators and saws for his own use for an indefinite period. I don't know why he did it, he's never done anything like it before. And it puts me in an awkward position. I....'

'The owner?' Kirsty interrupted him brusquely. 'Who is he?'

The man hesitated, then shrugged. 'I suppose you could find out easily enough. It's the Squire, Gyles Grantham.'

A frown between her brows, Kirsty looked at him in puzzlement. 'But why should he do this to us? Did he say why?'

Morris snorted. 'Not him, he's a close-mouthed bas ... man. He never lets you get friendly with him, or takes you into his confidence. Too much the Lord of the Manor for that.'

'You sound as if you don't like him?' Penny put in drily.

Shrugging, he said, 'I have to work for him, I can't afford to dislike him. But I'm sorry for your sakes. I'd have liked to help you girls, I really would, but there you are,' he spread his hands helplessly.

'Maybe you still can,' Kirsty told him. 'There must be other hire firms in the area. Can you give us their telephone numbers?'

'Well, I can, of course, but it wouldn't do you any good because the whole chain belongs to the Squire. He's bound to have anticipated that you'd try somewhere else and have given the order to all the centres. I'm just a cog in a big wheel, you see.'

Kirsty saw all right. She saw that for some unknown reason this Gyles Grantham had decided he didn't want them in Notley, and he had taken steps to start driving them out before they'd even moved in properly. But why? The only reason she could possibly think of was because she had outbid his agent for the cottage. But surely he couldn't be so cruel, so selfish as to. . . . Her thoughts froze suddenly. Turning to Alan Morris, she said, 'The Squire—what does he look like?'

He pursed his lips. 'Well, he's tall, about six feet two, I should think. Dark hair, aristocratic-looking sort of face.'

'Does her drive a Range-Rover?'

'Why, yes, he does. Why do you ask? Do you know him?' he asked curiously.

'No, it doesn't matter. Thanks anyway. We know it isn't your fault. Come on, Penny.'

They walked out into the dying rays of the winter sunshine, but Kirsty stared at the view unseeingly. Her mind was filled with the memory of the man who had watched them on the day they moved in, his face full of anger. And somehow she was quite sure that he and Gyles Grantham, the Lord of the Manor, were one and the same. She became aware that Penny was clutching her arm and talking to her, her face scared and miserable.

'Oh, Kirsty, what on earth are we going to do? Will we—will we have to go back to London?'

The look on Penny's face, when she had just begun slowly to come back to life, angered Kirsty uncontrollably. She put her hand over her sister's and said with impassioned resolve, 'No, we're not! We're staying here and we're going to make a success of it. We're going to get that garden prepared and ready for planting if I have to dig every foot of it myself!'

Penny stared at her in horror. 'But it's three acres!'

'It doesn't matter, I'm still going to do it, and I don't care what this man Gyles Grantham tries to do to us, *nothing* and no one is going to drive us out of Briar Cottage!'

CHAPTER TWO

THE next morning found them dressed in their oldest jeans and sweaters and brand new wellington boots, Penny's bright red, Kirsty's yellow. They were standing on the moss-covered patio at the back of the house and looking at the garden in some dismay. Bravely, Kirsty tried to hide her feelings by being extremely practical.

'I suppose the first thing we ought to do is to go over the whole ground and see if there are any plants we want to salvage, then dig over a part near the house which we can use as a kitchen garden to grow vegetables and things for our own use. Any plants we think we can use we can then transplant to that part.'

As they started walking over the ground, Kirsty began to realise the full extent of what they had taken on. The hedges were all overgrown and those that bordered the lane running alongside the cottage were almost lost beneath thick branches of entwining bramble that seemed to reach out and pluck at their clothes as they passed. There was a heavy, five-barred gate almost halfway along the hedge at the back of the garden, and when they looked over it they saw that the far side of the hedge had been cut expertly back. The Squire making sure that the hedge didn't encroach on to the field where the herd of Jersey cows grazed, Kirsty thought wryly. She knew next to nothing about farm animals, but even she could see that these were in beautiful condition as they moved, fat and contented, across the field, their bovine eyes turning to regard the girls impassively. They completed their exploration of the garden and were rewarded with gooseberry and blackcurrant bushes, a jungle of raspberry canes and a large area almost covered with strawberry plants.

'Good heavens, we'll never be able to use all that lot!' Penny exclaimed. 'What a shame to throw them away.'

Kirsty turned to her, her eyes sparkling. 'Why throw them away when we can sell them?'

'Sell them?'

'Why not? We'll dig up those plants we don't need for ourselves and put them out by the front gate with a notice saying they're for sale. We can certainly do with the money.'

Penny grinned. 'All right. I'll find something to put them in.'

Soon they had dug up about a hundred plants, their roots carefully packed round with earth, and had put them in a big box just outside the front gate. Penny had written a large notice: 'STRAWBERRY PLANTS. 10p EACH. A POUND A DOZEN' and fastened it on the hedge. They also put out a stick and an old tin tray they had found in the kitchen for the customers to bang to attract their attention while they continued working in the back garden.

They had several customers during the course of the morning and took it in turns to serve. Kirsty had an idea that most of the people buying the strawberries were doing so out of curiosity to see what the new owners of Briar Cottage were like rather than because they needed the plants, but she didn't mind, she wanted to get to know their neighbours and this was as good a way as any. They could hear the tray being banged again now and Penny stuck her fork into the ground.

'My turn. Hey, we're really doing a great trade,' she said excitedly, and ran off round the side of the house. But within five minutes she was back, the smile wiped from her face. 'Kirsty, you'd better come,' she said tremblingly. 'There's a man. He—he says we have no right to sell the strawberries. He says if we don't take them in at once he'll call the police and have us prosecuted.'

'What? But he can't . . .' She looked at Penny's white face and said angrily, 'Don't worry, I'll deal with him.' She slammed her fork into the ground and stalked round to the front of the cottage, jaw firmly set, eyes sparkling with annoyance.

A man was standing with his back to her at the open gate. He was wearing a shooting jacket over tan corduroy trousers and he had a beautiful red setter at his heels. The dog stood up as Kirsty approached and the man turned to face her. For a moment she faltered. She supposed she ought to have known. Who else but the high and mighty Squire Grantham would be so hateful as to threaten them with prosecution? Kirsty continued towards him, more slowly now. The manager of the garden centre had been right, he was autocratic-looking now she saw him close to. In his early thirties, she judged, he had a square, masterful face with a strong chin, dark, hard eyes that ran over her appraisingly, and a thin mouth that twisted with contempt at what he saw.

'So they sent you, did they?' he said scathingly as she came up to him. 'Too afraid to come and face me themselves. Or did they suppose that I would be diverted by a pretty face?' he added with a derisive sneer.

'They?' Kirsty looked at him in bewilderment. She

opened her mouth to go on, but he interrupted her brusquely.

'Well, they much mistook their man. And if you think I'm going to stand and watch you and your friends turn this place into a hippy commune, then you're wrong, dead wrong!'

'A hippy commune!' Kirsty stared at him in consternation, wondering where on earth he could have got that idea, but then she remembered that the hospital crowd had been with them when he saw them before and how it must have looked to him. She relaxed a little and tried to explain, but he swept on inexorably.

'You may have thought this the ideal place to practise your ideas of self-sufficiency, but let me tell you, young woman, we don't want any parasitic drop-outs in Notley. If I hadn't been away at the time of the auction and had to rely on an agent who was afraid to go over the verbal limit I'd given him, you'd never have had the chance. I would have made darn sure that your type never even got a foothold here.'

'Oh, and just what is my type?' Kirsty's face was pale, but she held herself in check.

'Do you really want me to define it for you?' asked Gyles Grantham sarcastically. 'Yours is the type that's incapable of holding down a job, who are too lazy and uncaring to make themselves a place in decent society and who think the whole world's against them. So they find a place like this and think that digging the soil and putting in a few seeds gives them the right to lead an immoral, unprincipled life. And practise a free-love philosophy, I don't doubt,' he added, his mouth curving into a contemptuous curl. 'But the worst part of it is that you contaminate the community around you, preach your perverted gospel to the village youngsters, so that they in turn become corrupted. But you're not going to get away with it in Notley! Whatever it takes, I'm going to make damn sure of that,' he finished vehemently.

Kirsty glared at him furiously, two bright spots of colour high on her cheekbones. The hold on her temper had long gone and with it any thought of telling this arrogant man how wrong he was. She wanted only to stab and wound him as he had her.

'Well, now you've so gallantly told me what you think of me, it's my turn to tell you a few home truths, Mr Dictator Grantham. Oh, yes, I know who you are,' she added at his flicker of surprise. 'Your tyrannical reputation has gone before you. We've only been here a few days and yet several people have already told us what a despot you are. Well, you may think you're God Almighty in this neck of the woods, Squire Grantham, but we're not some of your miserable tenants and employees, and if you think you can come here and harass us, then you're very much mistaken! You may have ordered your minions not to serve us, but we're going to make a go of this place whether you like it or not. So why don't you take yourself off and go and play at being a little tin god with someone who'll pander to your Hitler-sized ego by crawling and being servile to you? Just the way you like them,' she added nastily.

For a moment he stared at her, eyes blazing. 'Why, you insolent little minx! I ought to put you over my knee and give you the spanking you deserve,' he said savagely. 'Somebody should have taken you in hand years ago, then maybe you might not have turned out to be just a plaything for a bunch of unwashed hippies!'

'Anyway, at least they're young,' Kirsty retorted

recklessly. 'They're not perverted middle-aged men who get their kicks out of being sadistic to those less fortunate!'

At that he took an angry step towards her and Kirsty hastily backed away. 'You keep away from me! If you touch me I'll call the police.'

Gyles Grantham glared down at her balefully, looking very much as if he'd have liked to shake her, but then his expression changed. 'Go ahead, call the police,' he said scathingly. 'And while they're here, you can explain why you're selling goods without a retail licence.'

Kirsty gazed at him blankly, wondering what on earth he was talking about, and it was only when he gestured impatiently to the strawberry plants that she remembered why she had come out here in the first place. 'A retail licence? Just to sell a few strawberry plants? You must be crazy!'

'In your eyes, possibly. But I happen to be a justice of the peace, and I'm telling you that you need a licence.'

Disbelievingly she said, 'Are you trying to say that everyone who puts a few flowers or vegetables by their front gate has a licence?'

'No, I'm not. I suppose hardly any of them have. It's a law on which the authorities usually turn a blind eye.'

'But you, of course, being the amateur dictator that you are, intend to bring it into force against us,' Kirsty said disgustedly.

His eyes narrowed at her description, but he said merely, 'Yes, I do. If that sign isn't taken down at once I shall have the police round here. So now how do you like to be threatened?'

Baffled rage filled her. She was darned if she was

going to give in to him, but she dare not take the chance of getting mixed up with the police, not after Penny had so recently got into trouble. Something of her thoughts must have shown in her face, for a glint of triumphant malice came into Gyles Grantham's eyes. Perhaps it was this that made her brain start working overtime, because she suddenly had an idea. Fishing the fibre-tip pen they had used from her pocket, she took down the sign and began to write on the back of it in large capitals, her fair hair falling forward, her eyes intent. When she'd finished she said acidly, 'There. Now we're not breaking any laws.' And hung the notice up again.

The sign read: 'FREE STRAWBERRY PLANTS. THESE WERE 10p EACH, BUT SQUIRE GRANTHAM, IN HIS UNFATHOMABLE WISDOM, HAS REFUSED TO LET US SELL THEM TO YOU. ALL DONATIONS WILL, HOWEVER, BE GRATEFULLY RECEIVED. THANK YOU.'

It was Kirsty's turn to be triumphant now as she saw the look of tight-lipped anger on his face as he read it.

Malevolently he said, 'All right, young woman, smirk all you want to. You may think you've won this round, but I'm not going to rest until you and your friends are out of Notley and back in the London slums where you belong!' He turned abruptly and got into his Range-Rover, gunning it fast up the lane.

It was several minutes after he had gone before Kirsty could pull herself together. She found she was gripping the top of the rickety old gate tightly, her knuckles white but red-hot anger still pulsing through her in waves. Slowly she forced herself to relax, to take several deep breaths, but when she took her hand from the gate she found that it was shaking.

'Kirsty?'

She became aware that Penny was standing beside her, was looking at her worriedly, and had put her hand on her arm in the way she always did when she was frightened or needed reassurance. Automatically Kirsty covered it with her own and managed an unconvincing smile. 'It's all right, he's gone. I told you there was nothing to worry about.'

'Kirsty, I'm not a child, you don't have to pretend,' Penny said rather sharply. 'I heard every word. In fact, I wouldn't be surprised if half the village had heard, the way you were shouting at him.'

'Sorry,' Kirsty apologised. 'I did rather lose my temper, didn't I?'

'Yes,' her sister agreed with a little grin. 'I can't make up my mind which bit I liked best: the Hitler-sized ego, or when you called him a middle-aged pervert. I suppose you realise that after this he's *never* going to see reason?'

'He wouldn't have done, anyway,' Kirsty told her. 'Once that type makes up its mind about something, nothing and no one can change it. They're either too dogmatic or so conceited that they won't admit that they've made a mistake.'

They walked round the back of the house and decided to break for lunch.

'We're out of bread,' Penny remarked. 'We'd better walk into the village and get some from the shop.'

'If the Squire hasn't already ordered them not to serve us,' Kirsty said bitterly.

So it was with some misgivings that they walked down the road and round the green, but the friendly smile that the woman behind the counter gave them soon dispelled their doubts.

'You'll be the young ladies from Briar Cottage. Settling in, are you?'

It was obvious that the woman was curious about them, and Kirsty allowed herself to be drawn out. Perhaps if everyone knew they were harmless it might eventually filter back to Gyles Grantham, but she was very much afraid that what she had told Penny would turn out to be true and he would never relent towards them after this morning's episode. After they'd been there a few minutes the shop bell jangled behind them as a young man came into the shop. He was about twenty-six and dressed in a casual tweed jacket and trousers, but looked as if he had just been doing a rather dirty job, because there were still grease stains on his hands. He gave them a friendly nod and said good morning when he saw them, but Kirsty noticed that his eyes lingered on Penny. He bought some cigarettes and then left rather reluctantly.

'That's Dave Pagett,' the talkative shop assistant told them. 'He owns the garage just down the road. A very good mechanic, they say he is.'

She went gossiping on and it was some time before they were able to get away and go back to the cottage to eat their lunch of sandwiches and soup heated on the spirit stove.

'What are we going to do about the Squire?' Penny asked, voicing the thought that was uppermost in both their minds.

Kirsty shrugged helplessly. 'There's nothing we can do directly. Perhaps if he sees we're not doing any harm, he'll leave us alone. In the meantime I'll phone Simon and ask him to hire a rotovator in London for us and bring it down with him at the weekend if he can make it, or send it with the electricians if they're coming. I know it sounds like an awful lot of ifs, but that's the only thing I can think of, I'm afraid.'

'Sounds great to me,' Penny said heartily. 'That way we'll only have lost a week anyway.'

And Kirsty realised with some surprise that her young sister was trying to cheer her up and encourage her, which was a remarkable reversal of roles. They set to work again and she had plenty of time to think about her recent argument—no, let's face it—her stand-up row with Gyles Grantham. He was the most autocratic, overbearing man she had ever met, and he had brought out the worst in her. She didn't think she'd ever been so angry in her life before, and she had certainly never been so blazingly and unforgivably rude. But the wretched man had deserved every word of it; she had been more than willing to explain who they were, but he had been contemptuous from the start, his handsome face cold and unfriendly. Handsome? The word had come to her instinctively, but now that she thought about it she supposed that he was handsome in a hard, lean sort of way. Not by film-star standards, of course, his face was far too strong and forceful for that, and he certainly wasn't as good-looking as Simon. Good heavens, what was she doing comparing Gyles Grantham with Simon? One was the man she wanted very much to marry eventually and the other was her now undoubted enemy!

They worked on until it was almost too dark to see and were well satisfied when they stood back, tired and aching, and saw the amount of ground they'd cleared.

'That should be plenty for a kitchen garden,' Penny said. 'We'll leave it for a couple of days to harden off and then we can break it down and transplant all the things we want to keep.'

They ate another makeshift meal and then Kirsty left Penny working on the range while she dragged her tired limbs up the road again to the telephone box and put a call through to Simon.

'Hallo, darling, how are things going?'

'Not too well, I'm afraid.' Briefly she told him what had happened, but left out the row with the Squire. Somehow she couldn't bring herself to talk about it, her anger was still close to the surface and made her clench her teeth whenever she thought about him. 'Did you fix up for the electricians to come down?' she asked.

'Yes, they'll come on Friday evening and stay until they finish. They reckon it should only take a couple of days. And they'll bring everything they need with them.'

'Will you be able to come down yourself?' Kirsty paused. 'I—I'd be awfully glad if you could.'

She could almost see the expression on his face as he said understandingly, 'Need a shoulder to cry on?'

'Something like that,' she answered quietly, her eyes tight shut, her hands gripping the receiver as if it would bring him nearer to her, his strength and cheerfulness. Even just the sound of his voice was comforting.

'I'll try, Kirsty, believe me I'll try. But I'm down as stand-by surgeon in Casualty and it will mean getting someone to exchange with me.'

They talked on until Kirsty ran out of change and then she plodded wearily back to the cottage. But she didn't go in at once, instead leaning against the back wall and taking in the scents and sounds of the night. The smell of newly-dug earth came strongly to her nostrils and with it a strange feeling of satisfaction and achievement. Perhaps some primitive instinct in her needed the basic toil of tilling the earth. In her apartment she had always had plants and flowers all the year round. She grinned wryly to herself; perhaps she would turn out to be as keen a gardener as Penny. And Penny had certainly been happy today; it was one of the few times in the last month or so that Kirsty hadn't caught her gazing miserably into space, her face pinched and unhappy.

The gaunt, leafless branches of the trees cut the sky up into a jigsaw pattern as the crescent moon came out from behind a cloud and illuminated the garden. There was still a great deal to be done, but at least they had made a start. Her eyes naturally moved over the garden, and through the gap in the hedge she could just make out some pinpoints of light in the distance. Not the farm, because she couldn't see that from here, so it must be Notley Manor. She wondered what the Squire was doing now. Probably working out his next move in his battle to get rid of them, she wouldn't be surprised. Uneasily she wondered what it would be, but then shrugged the thought off. Sufficient unto the day. It was no use worrying, only time would tell her the bad news. She just prayed that they would have a breathing space in which to concentrate on getting the garden dug and to settle into the cottage better before she had to face him again.

But there was to be no respite. On Friday morning, just as they'd finished breakfast, an official-looking letter arrived and when Kirsty opened it she found it was from the local council. It was in very legalised language, quoting various Acts and local by-laws, but in simple terms boiled down to the fact that the council had been informed that their hedges were considerably overgrown and presented a menace to passers-by, and if they didn't cut them back within fourteen days of receipt of the letter, the council would have the work done themselves and send her the bill.

'Fourteen days!' Kirsty stared at it aghast. 'But there are yards and yards of hedges. And we need all our time this month to get the seeds in.' Slowly she lowered the letter, her mouth twisted with bitter cynicism. 'Gyles Grantham certainly didn't waste any time, did he? I bet he's the chairman of the council, or something. I'm sure they wouldn't have pushed this on to us within a week of our moving in, otherwise.'

'Well, we don't have time to worry about it now,' Penny pointed out practically. 'We've got the local chimney-sweep coming this morning and then we have to move the rest of the plants we want to keep and get the house ready for when the electricians come tonight. Okay, so the hedges have got to be cut back. We would have had to do it anyway, this letter just means that they'll get done sooner, that's all.'

That weekend and the following week were hectic. Both of them worked every minute of the day, falling into bed to sleep like logs and waking with their backs and muscles stiff and cramped and having to force themselves, groaning, to get up and start work again. But by the end of that time they had cleared and rotovated all down one side and along the back of the garden and had planted it with seeds and young plants which they had obtained from an established herb farm fifty miles away, taking an afternoon off to go and collect them. The beds for the various herbs had been laid out and neatly labelled. They had started off with a basic seven: sage, marjoram, fennel, basil, thyme, mint and rosemary, but intended to add lots more in April and May.

'We really ought to have camomile paths,' Penny remarked. 'All the Elizabethan herb gardens did.'

'But you have to cut that back all the time,' Kirsty objected. 'We need something more labour-saving.'

Penny thought for a moment and then turned excitedly. 'I know! How about the bricks taken from the inglenook? They would make wonderful paths if they were laid in patterns.'

'That's a great idea. I've been wondering what on earth we were going to do with those.'

Not only the garden but the cottage was also much improved. The electricians had done their work well and they now had hot water for baths instead of taking stand-up washes in water heated on the primus and carried up from the kitchen. Penny had finished the range and it now stood, repainted shiny black and with its brasswork gleaming, and although they could now plug in the electric cooker, they found it more economical to use the range, which they fed with logs of wood from the dead apple trees they had cut down. Simon hadn't been able to get down the previous weekend but was definitely coming this one and had promised to help them make a start on the hedges which they hadn't yet had time to touch. With three of them the job shouldn't take more than a couple of days, Kirsty estimated, and for the first time she began to allow herself to feel optimistic about the future. It seemed that, given a reasonable amount of luck, they were going to succeed with Briar Cottage, despite Gyles Grantham.

But that night, for the first time since they had moved in, it rained. Not just light rain, but a heavy downpour. Kirsty woke in the early hours to hear it driving against the window-panes and pulled her duvet closer around her, snuggling into its soft warmth, thinking that a shower of rain was just what they needed to make the seeds grow. Towards seven, however, she was woken by Penny calling her name.

'Kirsty, my bed is soaking wet. Ugh, it's gone right

through to my pyjamas!'

And when Kirsty looked she saw that water was dripping through the ceiling in several places and running down one corner of the wall.

'Oh, no!' Quickly they dressed and put buckets and bowls out to catch the drips, but when Kirsty went into the bathroom and the other bedroom she found that they were just as bad. 'The thatch must leak like a sieve,' she groaned. 'Heaven knows how much it will cost to have it repaired. It might even need rethatching.'

They wrung the wet duvet out as best they could in the bath; Penny was a heavy sleeper and must have been lying under the thing for hours before she woke up for it to have got as wet as that. They hung it over two chairs in front of an electric fire in the kitchen to dry out, but when they went to turn on the fire nothing happened and they found that all the electricity had fused.

'Oh, great! That's all we need,' Penny said dispiritedly, her teeth chattering with cold.

'Perhaps it's just as well,' Kirsty told her. 'Look, there's water coming through the light fitting on the ceiling. We might have got a shock or been electrocuted if we'd turned it on. Never mind, thanks to you we have the range. I'll get it going and make you a hot drink. You'll soon be warm.'

But when she went to get some logs from the neat pile they'd made by the kitchen door, she found that they were all soaking wet and refused to burn.

'Perhaps if I poured some paraffin on them,' Kirsty said doubtfully.

She got the can of fuel and tentatively poured some into the stove. They waited, but the logs still only smouldered weakly and threw up smoke, so she poured some more on, being more liberal this time. Nothing happened and she was beginning to wonder if there was any flame left to ignite the paraffin, when there was a sudden whooshing explosion and a circle of flames shot high out of the top of the range. At the same time the door at the front flew open and showered them with grime and smoke. Kirsty screamed and jumped backwards, knocking into Penny so that they both ended up on the floor, clutching each other in fright.

'The lid!' Penny shrieked. 'Put the lid on!'

Gingerly Kirsty crept forward and picked up the poker, reaching up to try and close the range. After two attempts she managed it and then stood up, shaking. The smell of the paraffin was everywhere and she saw that the can had fallen over and the liquid was glob-globbing out over the floor, and she must have crawled through it because it was all over her too. Slowly she looked round the room, filthy with smoke and soot, water dripping from the ceiling. Penny's duvet was grimed and a corner of it was resting in the evil-smelling pool of paraffin. They were cold, wet, and filthy dirty with no way to clean themselves up or get dry.

She sank into a chair. 'My God, it can't get worse than this!'

But even as she spoke they heard a peremptory knocking at the front door.

'Perhaps it's Simon, got here early,' Penny said hopefully.

Her untidy hair, soot-blackened face and dirty clothes forgotten, Kirsty rushed to the front door, her eyes alight with hope and anticipation. Simon would help them, would know what to do. But when she opened the door the look on her face changed completely. It wasn't Simon but Gyles Grantham who stood on the doorstep. His cold eyes swept over her, taking in every detail of her appearance, and he distinctly recoiled as the smell hit him. Oh Lord, now he really will think I'm an unwashed hippy, Kirsty thought despairingly.

'Miss Naylor?'

'Yes. What do *you* want?' she answered belligerently.

'I believe you received a letter from the parish council?'

'Well, you should know, you probably dictated it yourself,' she retorted.

His eyebrows rose. 'What gives you that idea?'

'You are on the council, aren't you? Probably the chairman, I shouldn't wonder.'

'As a matter of fact, I am. But it was the unanimous vote of the council members that you be warned about your hedges.'

Kirsty looked at him in unconcealed disgust, in no mood to mince words. 'What a pompous hypocrite you are! It's perfectly obvious that it was done at your instigation. Only a man like you would stoop low enough to use your official position to pursue a personal vendetta.'

She had the satisfaction of seeing him look rather discomfited for a second, but then his jaw hardened as he said, 'I came to find out whether you and your friends have any intention of carrying out the council's order, because if not I shall instruct the workmen to come and make a start.'

Kirsty glared at him. 'Aren't you rather jumping the gun? We were given fourteen days to do the job and we still have a week left. Sorry to disappoint you, Mr Grantham, but the hedges will all be cut by the end of next week,' she informed him sarcastically. 'You can try all you want to obstruct us, but we're already well ahead with our plans,' she added defiantly.

Raising his eyebrows, the Squire looked pointedly round at the untouched front garden. 'I see no sign of it,' he said, his mouth twisted in a cynical curl.

'That's because we get our priorities right,' Kirsty retorted, angered by his tone and eager to put him down. 'A good half of the land at the back of the house has already been dug and planted. Oh, yes, it's quite true,' she added when she saw the look of disbelief in his eyes. 'There are other places where rotovators can be hired, you know. So you see, it doesn't matter how much you try to stop us, because we'll always find a way round it. The sooner you realise that and leave us alone to. ...'

But he interrupted her angrily, his voice scathing, 'And the sooner you realise that you're not wanted in Notley and clear out, the better for you. It's no use trying to fight me because....'

'Fight! You don't fight,' Kirsty rejoined contemptuously, 'you just play dirty, underhand tricks. Now, get off my land before I have you arrested for trespassing.'

His face hardened. 'I'm beginning to get tired of the way you try to threaten me. You and your hippy friends might have formed some sort of idyllic picture about turning this place into a Garden of Eden, but I know your sort. In another month or so the novelty will have worn off and you'll be having wild parties with crowds of youngsters bedding down here and roaming around the countryside, stealing and picking fights with the local lads. Not to mention seducing the girls and getting them into trouble.'

At that a surge of red-hot anger swept through Kirsty's veins and she didn't care how she insulted him. Jeeringly she said, 'Oh, I see, that's what you're really worried about, is it? That they might cut you out so that you don't have a chance to seduce the girls yourself? You're living in the wrong century, Mr Grantham, you should have been born when the feudal lords ruled England. I bet you'd have really enjoyed putting down the peasants and chopping off the heads of anyone who thwarted you, not to mention having the right to go to bed with the women on their wedding night. Droit du seigneur, isn't that what they call it?'

'Why, you little....' He reached out suddenly and caught her wrist, pulling her towards him. His face was menacing as he said, 'I'm beginning to wish I had a few rights where you're concerned. I know why you've been made their spokeswoman, but every time you open your mouth you make it worse for yourself. If you think I'm going to let you....' He broke off suddenly and paused before saying in a completely different tone, 'What *is* that smell?'

Kirsty glared at him and pulled her wrist free. 'It's Chanel No. 5, I bathe in it every day!'

He stared down at her for a long moment, his dark eyes locked with hers as she gazed back at him defiantly. He seemed about to speak, but then changed his mind and turned to stride abruptly away.

Kirsty watched him go, baffled by his sudden departture, and it wasn't until Simon came through the gateway that she realised he had arrived. With a cry of pleasure she ran towards him. 'Oh, Simon, am I glad to see you!'

'Mm, likewise.' He kissed her warmly, oblivious to the smell. 'Who was that I saw leaving?'

Screwing up her nose, Kirsty replied, 'The Lord of the Manor himself. But never mind him. This morning has been just terrible, a whole series of disasters, but you'd better come in and see for yourself.'

His arrival seemed to give them renewed energy and somehow things didn't seem as bad as they had before. They bought lengths of plastic sheeting from the town and Kirsty helped Simon to fasten it to the roof beams under the thatch as a temporary measure to keep the rain out until they could afford to have the roof repaired, and by phoning up one of the hospital electricians they found out how to get the electricity working again. Penny cleaned up the kitchen as best she could and by the time she had finished there was only the smell of the wretched paraffin in the air to give any indication of the former mess.

It took ages to fix the plastic sheeting, especially over the gabled dormer windows, and they didn't finish until late on Sunday evening, so Simon decided to stay on that night as he wasn't on duty again until Monday evening. When they'd finished he suggested they walk over to the pub for a drink, but Penny complained of a headache and decided to go straight to bed. Slowly Kirsty and Simon walked along, hand in hand; the rain clouds had disappeared with the storm and the night was sharp and bright, the stars scattered across the sky like diamonds on black velvet. There was a wooden seat on the green set under a cherry tree, its tight buds giving the promise of bursting pink blossom. Simon led her to it and pulled her down beside him, putting his arm round her and kissing her lingeringly. A car came swiftly along the road, its powerful headlights illuminating them before Kirsty had a chance to pull free. She supposed it was inevitable that it should be a Range-Rover.

'Oh, no!' she groaned. 'That was the Squire's car. Now he'll think for sure that I'm a corrupting influence on the village.'

'Why should he think that?'

Briefly Kirsty explained and Simon frowned.

'He had no right to say that to you, of course, but maybe he's right in one way. Perhaps you ought to leave here.'

'Simon!' Kirsty stared at him in consternation. 'Not you too?'

He picked up her hand and toyed idly with her fingers. 'When you first told me about your idea for a herb farm I agreed that it would probably be the best thing for Penny.' He gave a shrug of resignation. 'Let's face it, I didn't have any right not to agree; I'm in no financial position to even look after you, let alone Penny as well, and I won't be until I pass my exams and get a decent position.'

He paused and Kirsty found herself holding his hand tightly—it was the nearest he had ever come to saying that he wanted to marry her.

Looking up, he went on earnestly, 'But I thought you would look for a place nearer London, somewhere that was already established and had decent living accommodation. To put it bluntly, Kirsty, I think you've taken on more than you can handle. Paying over the odds for the cottage and not having enough capital left to run it, is only asking for failure. You two girls just aren't strong enough to cope on your own, and quite honestly I don't feel like spending every free weekend I have in coming all the way down here and working for you, not to mention the effect that rough work could have on my hands. Okay, I know I wear gloves,' he said quickly as Kirsty went to interrupt, 'but my hands are my living, my whole future career, Kirsty, and I'm not going to take the risk of injuring them to try to prop up that house and give a little longer life to an enterprise that's doomed to failure.'

When she didn't answer he put his hands on her shoulders and turned her round to face him. 'Darling, I'm sorry, I know how much this means to you, but you won't be doing Penny any favours by staying here and seeing your plans fall to pieces. Look at it sensibly; you're on your own with very little money, the Squire doesn't want you here and will turn the villagers against you. You'll be unhappy and miserable and all for nothing. Better to cut your losses now and come back to London.' He put up his hand to push her hair back from her face. 'And I miss you, Kirsty,' he added softly. 'You don't know how much.'

'Oh, Simon!' For a moment she buried her head in his shoulder, but then straightened up determinedly. 'I'm sorry, but I'm not going to give up that easily. Everything was going fine until the storm. Now, thanks to you, the cottage is waterproof again. Oh, I know it looks terrible at the moment, but it could be a really nice house, and once we've got the garden straight we'll have time to work on it.'

'And the Squire? What about him and his threats?'

She shrugged helplessly. 'I can only hope that in time he'll realise we're not what he thinks and leave us alone.'

'And if he doesn't, if he goes on making your lives miserable?'

Her chin came up. 'I'm not going to let him push us out,' she said forcefully. 'If he thinks I'm coward enough to go running back to London just because he. . . .'

'I see.' Simon's voice had hardened. 'So you're staying because you're determined to fight him, even though I've begged you to come back?'

'No, Simon, it isn't only that. You know it's for Penny's sake. This man Grantham ... he just makes me furious every time I think of him, that's all.'

'He certainly seems to have had an effect on you,' Simon agreed wryly. But then, in a softer tone, 'All right, Kirsty, I can't force you.' He took her hands in his. 'But if you care about me at all, then promise me that if you haven't made a go of this place in six months you'll come back to London.'

Kirsty looked into his eyes, gazing at her so pleadingly, and didn't have the heart to refuse him.

'All right, Simon,' she answered rather tiredly. 'I promise.'

CHAPTER THREE

MONDAY dawned bright and clear and Kirsty got up early to see Simon off. His goodbye kiss was as warm as ever and she tried to return it as enthusiastically, but somehow she felt a slight reserve. Last night's conversation had altered their relationship subtly; he had demanded a promise from her that she had been unwilling to give, had more or less insisted that she choose between him and her sister when she wasn't yet ready to make that choice. Whereas before everything had been clear cut, now her loyalties felt divided; she wanted desperately to help Penny and yet by doing so she was in danger of losing Simon. All right, so he had given her six months, but that would soon pass and then she would be faced with having to make a decision, and whatever she decided someone was sure to be hurt.

Kirsty sighed heavily. It was just another worry to add to the list, and one she didn't have time to think about right now. Today the hedges were the number one priority and the sooner they made a start the better. Putting a cup of tea on a tray, she carried it upstairs to Penny. But her sister was slow to waken, and when she at last sat up, looked heavy-eyed.

'Are you all right, love?' Kirsty asked anxiously. 'You don't look at all well.'

'I've got a bit of a dry throat,' the younger girl admitted. 'But I expect I'll be all right when I've drunk this tea. Honestly, it's just a tickle,' she said reassuringly when she saw that Kirsty was looking at her doubtfully.

'Well, I hope so, because we must make a start on those hedges today.'

Kirsty left her to prepare breakfast and was relieved to see that Penny seemed fine when she came down later, dressed in jeans and sweater, which was almost a uniform to them now. They set to work immediately after breakfast on the evergreen hedge at the front of the house, each starting at a corner and working inwards towards the central gate. They soon found that it was so overgrown that they had to attack it with small handsaws and secateurs, and Kirsty soon had a pile of clippings beside her.

'I'll go and get the wheelbarrow to put them in,' she called to Penny. 'Then we can pile them up in the back garden and make a bonfire.'

They were too far away from one another to talk easily and so Kirsty concentrated on her work, cutting the hedge right back and lowering the height to about three feet, and it was only when she glanced across at Penny that she realised that she was sitting on the ground with her head in her hands. Quickly Kirsty dropped the saw and ran across to her.

'Penny, what is it?'

'Oh, Kirsty, I'm sorry, but I don't feel well. I've got the most foul headache and my throat's so sore.' Two large tears trickled down her face.

Distressed, Kirsty put her arm round her and helped her to her feet. 'Why didn't you tell me it was this bad? You should never have come out here.'

'But we've got to get the hedges done,' Penny answered fretfully. 'You know we can't afford any big bills.'

'And we can't afford to have you ill, either,' Kirsty told her forcefully. 'Come on, I'll take you inside and you go straight back to bed. And I don't want any arguments or I'll do my big sister act,' she threatened.

Penny managed a weak smile at this but was glad enough for Kirsty to help her into the cottage and fuss over her, pulling off her boots and dosing her with hot milk and aspirins before bringing her up a hot-water bottle and lighting the fire in the bedroom.

'At least we've got lots of twigs from the hedge to use as kindling,' she remarked cheerfully, but before she had got the fire going properly Penny was asleep, curled up under the duvet and clutching the hot-water bottle just as Kirsty remembered her clutching her teddy bear when she was a little child. As she looked at the younger girl, Kirsty felt her responsibilities weigh heavy on her shoulders; she could only pray that it was merely a cold, but she couldn't help worrying about the soaking Penny had had on the night of the storm.

Going back outside, she started work again, but made a point of going every half-hour to build up the fire and make sure Penny was all right, so the job didn't progress very fast. Towards two in the afternoon a car went by and then drew to a stop. A cheerful voice hailed her and she turned to see Alan Morris, the manager of the garden centre, walking towards her.

'Afternoon. See you're having a go,' he remarked unnecessarily. 'Settling down all right, are you?'

'Yes, thanks. Sorry I can't stop,' Kirsty replied, 'but I've got a lot to do.'

She bent to heap some more cuttings on to the wheelbarrow and then went to wheel it away.

'Here, let me do that for you.' Kirsty protested that she could manage; but he insisted on pushing it for her. 'No, it's no trouble. Where do you want it?'

'I'm making a bonfire in the back garden.'

He went away and seemed to be rather a long time

before he came back. 'See you've made quite a start at the back,' he remarked. 'Managed to get hold of a rotovator, did you?'

His eyes looked her over as he spoke and Kirsty squirmed inwardly, but then tried to pull herself together. Perhaps the man couldn't help it, perhaps he looked at everyone like that.

'Yes, some friends of ours hired one in London and brought it down for us,' she told him, wishing heartily that he would go away.

'Well, I've had a wasted journey, then,' Alan Morris said regretfully. 'I came over especially to tell you that I contacted a man I know who owns a rotovator, and he said he'd be willing to hire it out to you from this week. A private arrangement, of course—nothing to do with the Squire, you understand?'

He winked at her as he said this as if making her a member of a conspiracy, and Kirsty immediately felt contrite for having disliked him before. The man, however objectionable he was personally, was only trying to help them, and possibly at some risk to himself if Gyles Grantham ever found out, so her voice was warmer as she said, 'That was most kind of you. I really appreciate it, but, as you said, we don't need one now.'

'Oh, well, never mind. It was just an idea. I'll let the chap know. Suppose I'd better get back to work and let you get on with yours.' He stooped to put some cuttings in the wheelbarrow for her. 'It's yew, isn't it?'

'Is it? I'm afraid I'm terribly ignorant about plants and things yet,' Kirsty confessed.

'Well, next time you're free, just give me a ring and I'll come over and give you a few lessons,' Alan Morris leered at her.

She frowned, realising that she'd left herself wide

open to that one, but unable to make a biting retort because the man had only come here in an attempt to help them. 'Aren't you taking rather a risk standing here talking to me?' she reminded him. 'After all, the Squire could drive past at any moment.'

'Oh, no fear of that,' he rejoined with a sour smile. 'He's gone to a dairy show and won't be back for a few days.'

He went away at last and Kirsty thought wryly that his action in coming here hadn't been such a risky one after all. He was safe enough if Gyles Grantham was away.

When she went in to Penny again she found her awake, but her face was flushed and she complained that her throat felt worse, so Kirsty ran up to the shop and bought some lozenges and some packets of powder to make up into a lemon cordial. Penny refused to eat anything, but the cordial seemed to help, and Kirsty went reluctantly outside again, cursing at having to do the hedges when Penny needed her, and inevitably cursing the odious man Grantham for having made it necessary. She worked on until the front hedges were entirely finished, the clippings cleared away and the path swept. Only then did she make herself something to eat and sat down, her muscles aching in every part of her body.

When she'd eaten, Kirsty heated up some chicken soup and took it up to Penny, but the poor girl's throat was so sore that she could only manage a few mouthfuls before she lay back on the pillows exhausted.

'I can't, Kirsty. It hurts too much to swallow.'

'But you've had nothing since breakfast,' he sister said worriedly. 'Shall I make you something else?'

But Penny just shook her head listlessly and closed her eyes, too miserable to care. Feeling utterly helpless,

Kirsty refilled the hot-water bottle and made up the fire before getting ready for bed herself. Thankfully she crawled into it; her body seemed to be one big ache, but by far the worst was her right hand, which was red and sore from using the secateurs for so long. She fell asleep almost instantly, to dream of hedges reaching out to clutch at her, and woke with a start to find that Penny was calling her.

She had thrown off the duvet and was wet with perspiration. 'I'm so hot. My throat's on fire,' she croaked. 'Please can I have a drink of water?'

When Kirsty ran to get it for her she drank it down greedily, but then began to shiver instead and complain of feeling cold. Kirsty felt her forehead and found that her skin was burning hot, but all she could do was to dose her with more aspirins and sit beside her throughout the rest of the night, making sure that Penny kept covered up and holding her hand when she cried with the pain of her sore throat. Kirsty dozed fitfully, curled up in a chair, but as soon as morning came, got washed and dressed. Penny was asleep, but it was a fragile, restless sleep as she turned her head fretfully on the pillow, her breathing loud and painful. As quietly as she could, Kirsty went downstairs and pulled on her coat. She wasn't sure what time the local shop opened, but she thought it must be early because they also sold newspapers. A fresh wind whipped at the skirts of her coat as she ran along the road and she was out of breath by the time she got to the shop, but she was thankful to see that there were signs of activity inside.

The shopkeeper looked up in surprise as she hurried in. 'My, you're an early customer. Run out of matches, have you? That's usually what people want first thing in the morning.'

Kirsty leaned on the counter to recover her breath. 'Please, could you tell me the name of the local doctor?' she gasped.

'Someone ill, is there?'

'Yes, my sister. If you could give me the name so that I can go and telephone?'

'His name's Dr King, but there's no need to go over to the call box, you can use our phone. Here you are, here's the number.'

The woman led her through a door at the back of the shop into her own sitting-room and showed her the phone. Fortunately Kirsty got through, and after rather lengthy explanations about their being new in the district and not yet registered with a doctor, he finally agreed to come as soon as he could. She thanked the shopkeeper, but wasn't allowed to get away until she'd described Penny's symptoms and the woman had given her opinion of the illness.

'It's probably only a touch of 'flu. She'll be up and about in no time, you'll see.'

Kirsty thanked her again distractedly and ran home, passing the man from the garage who said good morning and then stared after her as she tore past him with only a shouted reply. Once back at the cottage, she ran upstairs and to her dismay found Penny sitting on the edge of the bed trying to pull her clothes on.

'What on earth are you doing? Get back in bed!'

'No. Must get up, got to help you with the hedges,' Penny mumbled, her eyes feverish in her flushed face.

'You're much too ill to go anywhere,' Kirsty returned firmly, taking the clothes away. 'I've sent for a doctor and he'll be here soon. Now get in my bed for a bit while I remake yours.' Quickly she changed Penny's bed, making it up with sheets and blankets instead of the duvet, and then helped her sister to wash and put on a fresh pair of pyjamas. Gently Kirsty brushed her hair and then helped her into bed again. Hurriedly she did the rest of the chores, relighting the fire and tidying the bedroom as best she could, looking round in despair when she realised how gloomy and cheerless it looked with its drab paintwork and un-curtained windows. Only the fire gave any warmth and cheer to the room.

But all her hurrying was wasted because the doctor didn't turn up until nearly eleven and then he only stayed for a short time. He examined Penny's throat and then wrote out a prescription.

'She's got a severe throat infection and a chill. Here's a prescription for some antibiotics. She'll need to stay in bed and be kept warm for at least ten days and to take it easy for another week or so after that, mind. I'll call in again tomorrow to see how she is.'

Kirsty thanked him and he hurried off on his round. The nearest chemist was in Barham, which would mean leaving Penny on her own, but it couldn't be helped. She hurried out to the van, but just as she was getting in an elderly woman came out of the cottage next door and called out to her. Kirsty turned as the woman approached and looked at her with interest; she hadn't seen their neighbour before and found her a small, birdlike woman with grey hair and spectacles.

'I see you've had the doctor round,' the woman be-gan without preamble. 'I used to be a nurse and I wondered if you wanted any help.'

'Why, that's very kind of you, Mrs . . .?'

'Mrs Anderson. I'm a widow woman.'

'I'm Kirsty Naylor, and my sister's name is Penny. I've got to go into Barham to get some medicine for her, but I'd be terribly grateful if you could spare the time to sit with her until I get back.'

'Oh, I can do that easily enough. You get on and I'll go and let myself in. Don't worry, she'll be all right with me.'

'I'm sure she will.' Kirsty smiled warmly at Mrs Anderson and drove into town much relieved. And when she got back with the medicine she found that the homely woman had taken over. Penny was propped up in bed with a cosy bedjacket round her shoulders and being fed with some milk pudding, and there was a delicious smell of meat casserole coming from the kitchen.

'I just thought I'd pop some of the stew I was making on to heat up for you,' Mrs Anderson told Kirsty comfortably. 'Now you're back I'll put in a couple of dumplings to go with it. You look as if you could do with a hot meal inside you.'

Kirsty grinned, fully aware that she was being mothered and not minding one little bit. It didn't take much persuasion to make their new neighbour stay and share the stew with her, and Mrs Anderson, being as 'interested' as the rest of the villagers, was soon finding out all about her, and in return told a lot about their neighbours. Kirsty enjoyed the chat, but began to feel fretful about losing time on the hedges.

In the end she said apologetically, 'I'm sorry, Mrs Anderson, but I really must get on now. The Squire has ordered us to cut our hedges by Saturday or else pay the council to do it.'

The little woman looked at her in some astonishment. 'The Squire has?'

'Well, officially it's the parish council, but it's definitely his doing.'

'That's not like the Squire. He's usually the first to offer to help anyone.'

'The natives of the village, perhaps, but obviously

he doesn't like newcomers.'

'It doesn't matter who it is. He encourages people to come here to keep the village alive, and he does everything in his power to help them. Why, this village would have died out if he hadn't fought to keep the bus service and found someone to run the post office.'

'It must be just us he's taken a dislike to, then,' Kirsty remarked rather tightly. 'But I've still got to get those hedges finished.'

She went ouside and looked in dismay at the hedge going down the side of the house. It was at least fifty yards long and much taller and more overgrown than the ones in the front, and it was also of a different wood, a thorny variety that was heavily entwined with brambles. It was so high that she couldn't reach the top and so she got out the step-ladder and resignedly set to work. The brambles continually caught at her clothing and scratched her skin until she put her heavy coat on, but even then the thorns sometimes dug through her thick gardening gloves and hurt her hands. She cursed the things and realised just why the place had been called Briar Cottage, but she worked relentlessly on, conscious of the time that had been lost and the amount still to do. Even as the light began to diminish she went on cutting the hedge back, loading the barrow and emptying it, almost like an automaton, her lack of sleep the previous night making her feel nearly drunk with fatigue, and she only gave up when it became so dark that she was in danger of cutting off her own fingers.

Penny was sleeping peacefully and the room was warm and cosy, thanks to Mrs Anderson popping in from time to time during the course of the afternoon, but there was still the linen from Penny's bed and the rest of the washing that she'd done that morning to be

ironed before she could go to bed. Kirsty picked up
the iron and nearly dropped it again; the sores on her
right hand had turned to blisters and the heat from
the iron cut into them like a knife. Covering the worst
ones with strips of sticking plaster, Kirsty put a glove
on her hand and by this means managed to do the
ironing, but she was heartily thankful when she had
finished and could go to bed. Penny had to be given the
antibiotics every four hours, so she carefully set the
alarm and dragged herself out of sleep to administer
the dose and reset the alarm, but this time she slept
only fitfully, almost as if she was waiting subconsciously
for the alarm to ring again.

Unfortunately the next day was Mrs Anderson's day
at the Oxfam shop and the one after that her Meals
on Wheels day, so Kirsty had to cope without her help,
looking after Penny and rushing out to work on the
hedge whenever the younger girl fell asleep and could
be left for a while, so that the days became a nightmare
jumble of hedge and cottage, and the nights of housework, ironing, and broken, unrestful periods of sleep
that left her feeling like a zombie in the morning.

But the hedge was slowly but surely being con-
quered. There had been one tricky part where it grew
close to the house and the thatch came down so low
that the brambles had started to bridge the gap and
Kirsty had had to pull them out carefully one by one,
but every day saw her nearing the neatly clipped-back
hedge that marked the point where her land adjoined
Gyles Grantham's. But on Friday morning her hand
was so sore that she could hardly hold the secateurs
properly; she dropped them and lost them in the thick-
ness of the hedge. She wasted some time trying to find
them before giving up and getting the pair that Penny
had been using, being careful to tie them on to her

wrist with a piece of string this time. These lasted for a few hours but then fell to pieces in her hands.

Kirsty gazed at them in consternation, hardly believing it. Darn! Now she would have to drive into town and buy another pair. By the time she got back it was raining hard and Penny called to her fretfully as soon as she got in. As patiently as she could, Kirsty saw to her needs, looking anxiously out at the weather and praying for it to stop raining; if she didn't get back out there soon she wouldn't be able to finish the beastly hedge in time. She realised that there wasn't a lot left to do, perhaps about twenty yards, which she could probably afford to pay to have done, but somehow it had become more than just a task to be finished by a certain time, it had turned into something personal between her and Gyles Grantham. She almost felt as if she was attacking him when she attacked the hateful hedge. She had sworn to him that it would be finished by Saturday and it was now a point of honour with her that it should be done by the time he got back from his dairy show, so that when he drove up the lane on his way home he would see for himself that she had beaten him.

Impatiently she stood at the window, drumming her fingers on the sill as she looked out at the grey skies. Then she made up her mind; a drop of rain wouldn't hurt her and she couldn't afford to waste any more time. Covering the sores on her hand with the last of the plasters, Kirsty forced the gardening glove over her swollen fingers and went back outside, a yellow rain hat pulled over her hair. Three hours later she was still standing on the step-ladder in the pouring rain, a flashlight balanced on the top step so that she could see what she was doing, when a car came round the corner, its headlights cutting paths of light through the darkness. It pulled up sharply just a few yards away and then the horn blared peremptorily, demanding a passageway. Slowly Kirsty began to descend the ladder, a wave of frustration almost overcoming her fatigue, because she knew instinctively who was in the car and knew that she wouldn't now have the satisfaction of finishing in time for a complete victory.

Reaching up, she took down the flashlight and closed the ladder, standing well into the side so that he could drive by, but suddenly the car door opened and Gyles Grantham crossed briskly towards her. Plucking the flashlight from her hand he shone it into her face, making her turn her head aside in protest.

'I *thought* so,' he said, his voice sounding angry. 'What the hell are you doing out here at this time of night?'

Resentment at his tone made Kirsty reply sharply, 'I should have thought that was obvious to the lowest intelligence! If you're going by, would you please hurry up. I want to get on with my work.'

'You don't seriously intend to carry on in the dark?' he asked in exasperated disbelief.

Kirsty tried to look at him, but he was still shining the flashlight into her face and she couldn't see.

'Yes, I do. Your ultimatum was that the job had to be finished by tomorrow, remember? And would you please take that flashlight away from my eyes?'

The light was lowered at once and Kirsty could see him now. He was wearing a military type trenchcoat that somehow seemed to make him more autocratic, the rain falling unheeded on his bare head. His eyes looked down at her balefully as he said, 'Why you? Why do they always leave you to do all the work?'

'That's none of your business,' Kirsty retorted. 'Now, do you want to get by or not?'

He muttered something savage under his breath and then shoved the flashlight back into her hand and strode back to his car, but to her astonishment instead of driving on up the lane, he reversed back the way he'd come and turned into the road out of her sight. Kirsty was left standing there feeling rather foolish, but within two minutes he strode briskly back and had taken the ladder from her, tucking it easily under one arm.

'Hey, give that back! You've no right to....' She tried to make a grab for the ladder but was encumbered by the flashlight, then she found her arm had been seized in a firm grip and she was being pulled, none too gently, towards the house. 'Let me go!' She struggled fiercely, but it was no use, his hand held her as securely as a vice and she was dragged along behind him, almost running as he strode along. 'Just what do you think you're doing?' she yelled at him furiously.

They had reached the back of the house before he bothered to answer her. He paused to prop the ladder up against the wall and then he yanked her roughly round to face him. 'All right, I'll tell you what I'm going to do,' he said forcefully. 'I'm making it my business to find out just why that bunch of idle hippies has left a girl to do all their dirty work. It wouldn't surprise me if they were all drunk out of their minds most of the time, or else high on drugs.'

He pulled her towards the door, but Kirsty hung back. 'It isn't like that at all. Please, you've got it all wrong. There's just the two of us, that's all there's ever been. It was only....'

But he interrupted her brusquely. 'Do you really expect me to believe that?' His eyes glittered down at her angrily.

Kirsty stared up at him. He had pulled her close

against him, his fingers biting into her arm. Slowly, tiredly, she said, 'No, I don't suppose I do.'

'Quite.'

Going into the kitchen, he closed the door behind them. For a moment he looked round, his eyebrows raised in disgust at the shabbiness of the room, then he went into the hall, still pulling her along. He took one look at the state of the sitting-room with its piles of rubble, said, 'Good Lord!' and shut the door again.

'*Now* are you satisfied?' she demanded.

'No, I'm not. There are still the upstairs rooms and I saw a light in one of them as we came in.'

'Don't you *dare* go upstairs!' Kirsty exclaimed hotly.

'Why? Frightened I might find out the sleeping arrangements?' he taunted.

'If you go upstairs I'll ... I'll....'

The grip on her arm tightened. 'You'll what?'

Kirsty bit her lip and looked away, unable to bear the mocking derision in his eyes, knowing that there was nothing she could do, even to scream for help would be useless and would only scare Penny, which was just what she was trying to prevent. He laughed and led her up the stairs.

First he looked into the room on the left of the landing, snapping on the light to let his eyes wander over the furniture they'd stored there. A quick glance into the bathroom and then he approached the door of the other bedroom. He must have felt some tension in Kirsty because he looked briefly at her before pushing open the door and stepping inside. Penny lay fast asleep, her hair tousled on the pillow, and Kirsty gave a sigh of relief that she wouldn't be frightened by a man charging into her room. Wrenching her arm from Gyles Grantham's suddenly slack grasp, she waited until he had come out of the room and shut the door behind him, then she turned abruptly and preceded him down the stairs and into the kitchen.

She found that she was still carrying the saw and the flashlight and put them down on the table before turning to face him. Trembling with emotion, she said, 'You've seen what you came to see, now get out of my house!'

'Look, Miss Naylor, I....'

'No, *you* look! What right do you think you have to come here and—and *rampage* through my house? Just because you own near enough everything round here it doesn't mean that you can walk in where and when you choose. I told you there were only the two of us, but even if there had been a crowd it wouldn't have been any of your business; we have the right to lead whatever kind of life we want, without interference from you or anyone else,' she finished furiously, leaning forward with her hands flat on the table to emphasise her words.

'There were others here, I saw them.'

'All you saw were some friends who came down that first weekend to help us move in. They went back to London the next day.'

'And the following weekend? There were more men here again then.'

Kirsty stared at him in loathing. 'My God, you really do like spying on people, don't you? They were electricians. They came down to rewire the house for us.' She straightened up, not waiting for him to answer. 'Now get out of here. Go on, get out!' she almost shouted when he hesitated.

For a moment longer he looked at her, tight-lipped. Their eyes met, Kirsty's hot with fury, while his were frowning in baffled exasperation. Then he gave a small, frustrated shrug and went to walk past her, but he stopped suddenly, his glance fixed on the table. Kirsty followed his eyes and saw a large smudge of blood where her right hand had rested.

'You're hurt. Here, let me see.'

He went to take hold of her hand, but Kirsty quickly put it behind her. 'It's nothing. I'm waiting for you to go.'

'Not until I've seen for myself. Let me look at it.'

'No!' Briefly she defied him, trying to pull away as he caught hold of her arm, but then her hand knocked against the table and it hurt so much that she gave a cry of pain and he was able to seize her wrist.

'You stubborn little fool! Now hold still while I take this glove off.'

He started to ease the bloodstained glove over her fingers and she had to quickly turn her head away so that he wouldn't see the tears of pain that came to her eyes. She wouldn't let the beastly man see her cry, she wouldn't!

'I'm going to have to cut it off. Do you have any scissors?'

'In—in that box on the table.' She tried to keep her voice steady, but he looked at her sharply. Reaching up, he pulled the rain hat from her head so that her hair cascaded down about her shoulders and her eyes were no longer shadowed. His eyes rested on her face as if he was seeing it for the first time, running over her features one by one and coming back to her eyes, set wide under level brows and misty now with pain. Then abruptly he turned and reached for the scissors.

He took one look at her hand after he had cut off the glove and exclaimed, 'What on earth have you done to it?' Without waiting for an answer, he went over to the sink and filled the electric kettle. 'Is this all your medicine kit?' he asked, indicating the box.

Kirsty nodded, not trusting herself to speak.

Putting some antiseptic into a basin of water, he began to swab her hand with cottonwool, his hands gentle. 'You haven't answered my question,' he reminded her without looking up. 'How did your hand get into this state?'

'The secateurs made blisters. I kept putting plasters on them, but they must have come off today when the glove got wet.'

Pausing in what he was doing, Gyles Grantham raised his head to look at her. His voice tight, he said, 'Are you telling me that you two girls cut all that hedge by yourselves?'

'No, I did it by myself,' she answered on a note of defiance.

'But your sister? Surely she helped?'

Kirsty shook her head. 'She's ill. The roof leaked in the storm and she caught a chill when she got wet.'

He frowned, his eyes searching her face. 'You did all that alone?'

'Yes.'

'Couldn't any of your friends have helped you?'

'Simon did come down, but we spent the whole weekend lining the roof with plastic sheeting.'

'Simon?'

'My boy....' She stopped, then finished sarcastically, 'One of my hippy friends. And you've changed your tune, haven't you? One minute you're bursting in here trying to drive them out, the next you're asking why they're not here, helping us.'

To her surprise his mouth twisted into a wry grin. 'Touché!' Looking down at her hand, clean now and with the sores exposed, he added, 'And if I needed anything to convince me that I was wrong, I have only to look at your hand to realise just how mistaken I've been.'

He looked at her earnestly as he spoke, but after a quick glance at him Kirsty flushed and turned her head away, her hand starting to shake in his. His jaw tightened, but he said nothing further and concentrated on deftly bandaging her hand.

When he had finished he started to clear the things away, but Kirsty said hastily, 'There's no need to do that, I can manage.'

'It's no trouble. Where do you keep your coffee?'

Automatically she answered, 'There's a jar in the cupboard,' then added sharply, 'Look, I can make my own coffee, thanks. I'm grateful to you for doing a Dr Kildare act on my hand, but I'm sure you want to get home, so please don't let me keep you.'

Setting two mugs on the table, he raised his eyebrows quizzically. 'Now anyone who was at all sensitive might infer from that that you didn't want me to stay and have coffee with you.'

'And they would be right. Why don't you wait until you're invited?'

Again that twisted smile. 'If I'd done that I would never have found out the truth about you, would I?'

Kirsty had no answer for that one and she stayed silent while he finished making the coffee. He raised an eyebrow. 'Do you think we might sit down?'

'Why bother to ask? You seem always to do what you want, anyway.'

She struggled to take off her raincoat, but the thick PVC material was difficult to unbutton with her left hand.

protest he was close beside her and unbuttoning the coat to slip it off her shoulders. He had taken off his own trenchcoat to reveal a suede jacket over a cream

polo-necked sweater. He seemed very lean and powerful as he stood so close and Kirsty realised that he was
very fit, his body hard and muscular, but it was his
complete self-assurance, his sheer masculine domin-
ance, that made her turn quickly aside and take a chair
well away from him on the other side of the table. If
he noticed he gave no sign, merely hanging her coat on
the back of the door and seating himself casually
opposite her, his legs stretched out in front of him and
crossed at the ankles.

For a few minutes they drank in silence and then
the Squire asked, 'Is you sister very ill?'

'No, she's over the worst.'

He looked at her thoughtfully. 'Why didn't you put
me right about your friends before? Why let me go on
believing they were hippies?'

Kirsty shrugged. 'You wouldn't have believed me if
I had. You didn't believe me tonight until you'd seen
for yourself. And anyway,' she hesitated for a moment,
but then thought, oh, what the hell. 'You made me so
mad that I didn't care what you thought of us. In my
book anyone who could try and drive us out the way
you did just isn't worth caring about. It was mean and
underhand and rotten. So now, Mr Grantham, you
know exactly what I think of you.'

She glared at him defiantly, but to her surprise he
didn't rise to the bait and get angry at her rudeness as
she expected him to. Instead he set down his empty
mug and stood up.

'Oh, I already knew that, you did happen to mention it in passing once or twice before.'

Kirsty, too, came to her feet. 'So why don't you just
go away and leave us alone, which is all we wanted in
the first place?'

Picking up his coat, he put it on, tying the belt in a

casual knot instead of buckling it. 'Don't worry, I'm leaving. But I'm afraid I'm not going to promise to leave you alone; whether you like it or not you're going to need help if you're going to get this place on its feet.'

Kirsty looked at him balefully. 'You're the last person I'd ever turn to for help. I'd rather go under!'

His eyes narrowed and for a moment he looked angry, but whatever retort he had been going to make he bit back, saying merely, 'You're tired out. Go to bed, child, and take care of that hand.' And then he was gone, the door shut quietly behind him, leaving Kirsty with a jumble of mixed emotions that she was too exhausted to try and analyse.

CHAPTER FOUR

The alarm went off as usual the next morning and Kirsty quickly reached out to turn it off before it woke Penny, then she snuggled back under the covers for another five minutes and promptly fell asleep again. So it was late before she had taken care of Penny's needs and was able to think about the hedge. The thought of having to spend the whole day trying to get it finished made her feel terribly dispirited, especially now that she was no longer driven by the urge to be done before Gyles Grantham came back. Still, there was no help for it. Forcing her hand into a new glove, she retrieved the step-ladder from where he had left it the night before and carried it through the garden.

The weather had changed completely overnight as only the weather in Britain can. Today it was warm and sunny, birds sang in the branches of the apple trees and some bulbs in the front garden were beginning to push aside the weeds. It was the kind of day when it was good to be young and alive, when you thought about packing away your winter woollies and getting out your summer dresses. At this thought Kirsty looked at her grubby working clothes and gave a rueful grin; pretty dresses were definitely out for her for quite a while.

Going out of the gate, she began to walk briskly down the lane, but then her footsteps slowed as she stared at the hedge. Where she had expected to see ten yards or so still waiting to be done, it was now uniform and even. She stared at it in perplexity; surely she couldn't have come to the end last night without realising it? Admittedly she had been exhausted, but not that dead on her feet. As she walked further along, Kirsty saw a definite line where someone else had taken over. The difference was so marked that it made her part look ragged and clumsy, whereas the last few yards looked so neat that she strongly suspected it had been done by a machine. The road had been swept too, and the clippings cleared away. It didn't take much imagination to realise who was responsible; there was only one man who had the facilities and labour available to do the job so quickly. Gyles Grantham had said that he was going to help her whether she liked it or not, and he had started with a vengeance. But he was right about one thing; Kirsty didn't like it, not one little bit!

Shouldering the ladder again, she began to walk back to the house, wondering grimly how many men it had taken to finish the hedge before she had even got up that morning. Briefly she speculated on whether he had foreseen her resentment at his high-handed action and had made sure that the job was done before she could interfere, as she most certainly would have done if she'd known about it.

She was still simmering with anger all that day, and having the time now to catch up on the housework did nothing to alleviate it. There were several reasons she could think of why Gyles Grantham had taken it on himself to help them, and none of them appealed to her. If he had done it as a sort of atonement for being wrong about them and now expected everything to be all square between them, then he was dead wrong, because Kirsty wanted nothing to do with anyone who had been as hateful as he had been. She was more inclined to think, though, that he had done it simply to make her feel grateful to him, but if that was what he wanted, she thought as she poked viciously at the coals in the range, then he was in for a rude awakening. And that evening she sat down and wrote him a terse letter informing him that the hedge was her property and that if he, or any of his employees, touched it again she would report the matter to the authorities. Which authorities she hadn't the faintest idea, but when she'd finished she looked at the letter with some satisfaction; that would show him that she meant what she said.

Kirsty supposed he must have got the letter, but she received no reply and didn't know whether to be pleased or sorry. A couple of times she caught a glimpse of him going by in his car, and, now that the hedge was cut, she saw him go up the lane on horseback, his dark hair hidden under a riding-cap. He looked towards the cottage as he passed, but Kirsty hastily whisked herself away from the window and she didn't think he'd seen her, but she found the idea of him being able to look into the garden vaguely disturbing.

Penny's health improved every day and she soon became fretful for something to do while she was tied to the house, so Kirsty drove into Barham and bought some pretty material to make curtains for the bedroom. She cut them out, and Penny, who was good with a needle, sewed them up on the machine. Unfortunately, though, they made the rest of the room look even shabbier and made Kirsty realise that she'd just have to start decorating. With the help of a book from the mobile library, she made a start in the other bedroom, stripping the walls and paintwork and repairing the cracks. By dividing her time between this and the garden, she found that the days just flew by and a fortnight was gone before she knew it.

April was a beautiful month, and for the first time

in her life Kirsty was in the countryside and able to
watch the spring unfold around her. She thrilled when
birds built their nests in the garden and didn't mind
that they pulled out pieces of the thatch to make them
with. Diligently she planted tarragon, chives and
parsley, and ran excitedly to tell Penny when she saw
the earlier seeds they'd sown coming through strong
and healthy.

Thanks largely to Mrs Anderson, she got to know
more of their neighbours and struck up a friendly
acquaintance with Dave Pagett, the owner of the garage, when she took the broken secateurs there to see if
he could fix them.

He took the pieces from her and said, 'You must
have lost the nut off the back. If you wait I'll see if I
can find one that fits.' After rummaging around in a
box he eventually found one and put the tool back
together again. 'How's your sister now?' he asked.
'They told me in the shop that she was ill.'

'Much better, thanks. But she's still got to take it
easy for quite a while yet, and I'm afraid she gets
rather bored when I'm working in the garden.'

The young man looked up. 'Perhaps she'd like some
magazines to read, then? I've got a pile of *Reader's
Digests* she could have, if you think she'd be interested.'

'I'm sure she would,' Kirsty replied, smiling warmly.
'We've got nothing but seed catalogues and she's been
through those about ten times already.'

He laughed at her exaggeration, his friendly, good-
looking face breaking into a broad grin. 'I'll get them
for you, if you'd care to wait a few minutes while I
wash my hands. I only live upstairs in the apartment
over the garage.'

He went to move away, but Kirsty said impulsively,
'Look, don't bother now. Why don't you bring them

round yourself later on? This evening, perhaps? I'm sure Penny would love to have someone other than me to talk to for a change.'

'Okay. I'll do that.' He seemed pleased at her suggestion and promised to call about eight, refusing to take any money for repairing the secateurs.

Penny, however, wasn't very pleased when Kirsty told her. 'Oh, no, Kirsty, how could you? I look terrible and my hair's a mess.'

But after Kirsty helped her to wash her hair and blow-dried it for her, she consented to make some scones, and then got carried away and made a couple of dozen cakes, some shortbread, and a quiche as well.

'Mmm, delicious!' Kirsty came in from the garden at tea-time and helped herself to a piece of shortbread still hot from the oven.

Penny pretended to slap her hand and said, 'Leave it alone. You're worse than a child!' And they both burst out laughing.

Kirsty licked her fingers and said, 'Seriously though, you really are a good cook. Much better than I am.'

'It's the range, it's tons better than an electric cooker.' Penny glanced wistfully out of the window. 'I can't wait to get outside in the garden again, I feel so frustrated not being able to help you.'

'You must get your strength back properly first,' her sister warned her. You were very low when—when we came here, otherwise your illness wouldn't have pulled you down so much.'

Penny's face became bleak. 'You mean when I was made a fool of by a married man. Why don't you say it? We both know that it completely messed up both our lives,' she said with bitter self-reproach.

Kirsty came to put an arm round her. 'For a little while, perhaps. But I certainly don't feel as if my life is messed up now,' she said stoutly. 'I wouldn't have missed this spring for anything, especially as everything seems to be going right for us now.'

'I wonder why. Perhaps the Squire's just biding his time and will spring something really nasty on us,' Penny said pessimistically.

'Oh, I think we've seen the last of him,' Kirsty reassured her. 'Now that he knows there are only the two of us and we don't hold regular orgies every weekend, that is.'

Penny looked at her in surprise. 'He knows? I wonder who told him.'

'Well, as a matter of fact, I did. We sort of met— well, not met exactly, it was more of a head-on collision —when you were ill.'

'What did he say?' Penny asked, intrigued.

'Well, he didn't go so far as to apologise, of course, but he admitted that he'd made a mistake while at the same time implying that it was my fault for having misled him in the first place,' Kirsty told her lightly.

'And he promised to leave us alone?'

'Not exactly. He seemed to think that we needed taking under his wing, but I told him in no uncertain terms that we weren't interested. That's one hen whose wing I definitely don't want to be taken under.'

Penny gurgled with laughter. 'Haven't you got your genders wrong? You mean rooster, surely?'

Kirsty looked at her in comic surprise. 'Yes, I suppose I do.'

Dave Pagett's visit was an unqualified success. He had an easy, pleasant manner and they soon felt completely comfortable with him. He stayed for a couple of hours and sampled all Penny's cooking, bringing a flush to her pale cheeks when he enthusiastically complimented her. It was obvious to Kirsty from the start that he was interested in the younger girl, and he put himself out to draw her out so that Penny was soon talking eagerly about their plans and laughing at his jokes, but it wasn't done in a blatant way and Kirsty at no time felt as if she was playing gooseberry. But she looked on this new development with mixed feelings; there was nothing she wanted more than for Penny to be happy, and Dave seemed nice and sincere enough, but she was also terribly afraid that her sister might get hurt again. Tonight, however, she was content to let things take their course. It was sufficient that Penny had some colour back in her cheeks and was happy and laughing like the teenager she was.

The next day Penny insisted that she was well enough to go for a walk, and it was so warm and fine that Kirsty agreed straight away. They set off down the lane and found a stile leading into a meadow that sloped upwards to a hill. It was so warm that soon they had taken off their jackets and walked along in just their skirts and blouses. They had gone only about a quarter of a mile, however, before Penny stopped to rest.

'Phew, this hill is steeper than I thought!'

'Are you sure you're all right?' Kirsty asked anxiously. 'You look exhausted. I really think it would be better if we went back. After all, it is your first day.'

However much she hated to admit it, Penny had to agree that she'd had enough and they retraced their steps, but at the stile Penny turned and said, 'Look, I know you were looking forward to this walk, so why don't you go on alone? I can manage perfectly well from here. I shall just sit in the lounger in the sun and probably fall asleep.'

'But I ought to come back with you and....'

'I can manage, honestly.'

This last was said a little snappily, so Kirsty didn't argue any further. 'All right, I'll see you later. Save me some scones for tea.'

She set off across the meadow once more, the sun warm on her bare arms. It felt good to wear a skirt again; the pretty pale blue material falling from a gathered waist made her feel feminine for the first time in weeks. It was too early for most wild flowers, of course, but there were plenty of dandelions and colts-foot among the new grass, and Kirsty thought that per-haps she might bring a basket some time so that she could gather the flower heads and make some dande-lion wine. Penny, she knew, would enjoy doing that. There was another stile at the end of the meadow and she climbed nimbly over into a piece of open country. The hill was steeper here and she was panting a little by the time she reached a thick copse of trees perched, rather incongruously, right at the top.

From here she had the most superb view of the countryside. She could see Briar Cottage nestled in the valley, and past it the village looked peaceful and serene as it slumbered in the afternoon sunshine. The only sounds were those of tractors working in the fields and the bird songs that had become so much a part of her everyday life now that she hardly noticed them. Her glance swept on and came to rest on the Manor. She could see it properly from here, and real-ised that it was much larger than she had thought, with a wing at each end of the back of the house and also several out-buildings in the beautifully laid out grounds. She studied it for some time; it looked so solid and timeless, as if all the world-shattering events that had taken place since its erection were mere casual in-trusions that had hardly touched the peace and pros-perity of the place.

Had Gyles Grantham's family owned the estate very long? she wondered. For a moment sheer envy filled her at the thought of knowing one's ancestry for hundreds of years, of having roots that were solidly planted in this beautiful English valley and of having one's name forever stamped across the pages of history. Had Granthams fought in the Civil War? Had their menfolk put to sea with Drake and Nelson?

Kirsty gave herself a mental shake; no good envying someone else's past when she had her own future to think about. She wandered along the edge of the trees, found some violets nestling among the undergrowth and was unable to resist picking a few and putting them in the top buttonhole of her blouse. There was a stretch of smooth ground at one point and she lay down on it in the sun, chewing a piece of grass and letting her mind wander.

She had phoned Simon regularly a couple of times a week, but he had made no mention of coming down to the cottage, instead suggesting that she come up to London for a weekend when Penny was better, and Kirsty was beginning to suspect that he wanted to show her what she was missing and pave the way for her to go back there permanently. Eventually, she knew, she would be faced with a decision: if she wanted to marry Simon she would have to leave Briar Cottage, and that meant selling up and taking Penny back to London with her, or else leaving her sister here alone to run the herb farm. Kirsty sighed wearily, turning the problem over and over in her mind. Why did life have to be so complicated? And she was still worrying about it when she drifted off into sleep, the sun enfolding her like a blanket.

The sound of a horse's hooves woke her, and for a moment Kirsty couldn't think where she was, but then the gentle snorting sound of the animal close by brought her fully awake and she sat up quickly. Gyles Grantham was sitting astride a beautiful palomino which pawed impatiently at the ground only a few yards away. His eyes ran over her, taking in her tousled hair and rumpled clothes. Kirsty suddenly realised that her skirt had ridden quite a long way up above her knees and she hastily pulled it down.

His eyebrows rose mockingly. 'I didn't realise I was going to find Sleeping Beauty up here.'

She got quickly to her feet, immediately on the defensive. 'Don't you mean Beauty and the Beast? And I'm *not* referring to the horse!'

To her surprise he laughed, and it was like coming face to face with a complete stranger; his eyes crinkled up at the corners and he seemed somehow younger and more human. Kirsty was so taken aback that she hardly realised that he had dismounted and left the horse to graze until he crossed the grass towards her. She immediately backed away.

'I suppose this is your land and you've come to order me off?' she said challengingly.

Leaning against a tree trunk, Gyles casually took a cigarette case from the pocket of his sports shirt and offered her one. They were most unusual cigarettes, black instead of white, and with a gold band just below the filter, she noticed. Silently she shook her head, watching him coldly. He shrugged and took one himself, drawing on it slowly before he answered.

'As it happens the land does belong to me, but you, and all the rest of the villagers, are welcome to walk here as often as you wish. And *I* don't send out letters telling people to keep away from my property,' he added sardonically.

Kirsty's chin came up. 'I told you I didn't need your

help and I meant it. I could have managed perfectly well alone.'

His mouth twisted cynically. 'How's your hand, Kirsty?'

Flushing, she looked away, then realising what he had called her, said angrily, 'I don't remember giving you permission to use my name.'

'You didn't.' Dropping the cigarette, he carefully ground it out under his heel. 'But as we're neighbours and will obviously be seeing a lot of each other, it seems reasonable for us to be on christian name terms.' He came nearer and his left eyebrow rose quizzically. 'Or are you going to persist in this childish attitude you've adopted?'

'How dare you? I am not a child!'

He let his eyes run slowly over her in open appraisal. 'You certainly don't look like one,' he agreed.

At that the fragile hold on her temper snapped and Kirsty raised her hand to slap his face, but he caught her wrist and his features hardened.

'And when you start behaving like a responsible adult maybe you'll get treated like one!' For a moment his dark eyes glared angrily down into her violet ones, then he gave an exasperated sigh and let go of her wrist. 'Look, I know we started off on the wrong foot and no one regrets that more than I do. But if you think I'm going to beg your forgiveness for putting obstacles in your way, then you're mistaken. I'd do the same again if I thought there was any danger to this village. Most of the people here are my tenants and I do my best to take care of my own. I thought you and your friends constituted a threat and so I acted accordingly. If you'd behaved like an adult and told me the truth straight away, I'd have been more than happy to welcome you to Notley.' He paused, trying to read her expression, but Kirsty was looking at the ground, her eyes veiled behind her lashes. 'So let's start again, shall we? Admit that we both over-reacted in the heat of the moment, but blame it all on the circumstances prevailing at the time.'

Kirsty didn't answer for several minutes, then slowly raised her eyes. 'All right, I'm willing to give it a try.'

Gyles gave a rather crooked grin. 'Meaning that you're going to reserve judgment until I've proved myself a friend instead of an enemy, I suppose. Well, it's a start at least.' Abruptly he changed the subject, putting out a long finger to touch the violets at her breast. 'Do you like flowers?'

Startled, she replied, 'Yes, of course. I love them.'

'Then you'll like what I have to show you. This way.'

He led the way round the edge of the trees, but when he started to walk along a narrow path that led into the depth of the wood, Kirsty hung back uncertainly.

Seeing her hesitation, Gyles looked at her in exasperation. 'It's all right, you're quite safe. Today's Tuesday; I only rape the village maidens on Fridays!'

Kirsty's eyebrows flew up and then she gave a reluctant laugh and moved to follow him again, but he seemed in no hurry to go on. Instead he stood looking down at her enigmatically. 'I was beginning to think you'd never do that.'

She gave a little frown of puzzlement. 'Do what?'

'Smile. You should do it more often.' His eyes looked deep into hers. 'It's like the sun coming out after rain,' he said softly.

Hastily Kirsty looked away. 'What is it you want to show me?' she asked coldly.

Immediately he turned and led the way further into

the wood, along a path so narrow that she wouldn't have noticed it herself. The trees grew close together here, letting little sunlight through, and the undergrowth was left to grow dense and unchecked, the trunks of long-dead trees allowed to lie where they had fallen. But presently Gyles said, 'Here we are,' and moved aside so that she could see past him.

'Oh!' She gave a gasp of pleasure and surprise. They had come to a clearing in what must almost be the centre of the wood, and here the sunlight shafted down on to a small brook, its waters rippling over stones. But it was the mass of flowers that grew on its mossy banks that made Kirsty catch her breath in wonder. The place seemed to be carpeted in the deep mauve of violets, but among them were drifts of delicate primroses and deep yellow celandines, and further back among the trees wood anemones lifted their star-like heads and grew so thickly that they looked like snow against the rich brown of the earth. Slowly she moved forward, afraid of treading on the flowers, her face lit up with delight at the beauty of the scene.

'Don't you want to pick some?' Gyles' voice brought her back to earth and she realised that she had been just standing and gazing her fill for several minutes.

She shook her head. 'No, that would be a kind of sacrilege. Do many people know about this?'

'Very few. I try to keep it as quiet as possible. Unfortunately most townspeople wouldn't appreciate the beauty of the place and would probably start uprooting the flowers, especially the primroses, and taking them to plant in their own gardens instead of leaving them here where they belong.'

Kirsty's voice hardened. 'How do you know I wouldn't do that? I'm a townperson.'

He glanced at her. 'You said you loved flowers. And

besides, you're not a Londoner any more now, you're a villager. You'll find that you will gradually be absorbed into the community and become so much a part of it that you'll forget you ever lived anywhere else. You'll know everything there is to know about your neighbours and they'll know all about you, much more than you'd believe possible. They will always be on hand to help you if you need it and they'll expect you to give unstintingly of yourself to them.'

He had spoken lightly, but there was an undercurrent of warning in his voice, and he looked at her intently as he asked, 'Do you think you can take it?' When she didn't answer straight away he added caustically, 'Or is this herb farm idea just some whim that you intend to give up when you grow tired of it?'

Kirsty turned on him, annoyed that he should disrupt the peace of such a perfect place, and her anger intensified because she wasn't sure enough in her own mind to give him a definite answer. 'What's it got to do with you? Why are you so interested in my affairs?'

Her voice rose in resentment and must have triggered off a similar reaction in Gyles, because he took a hasty step towards her, regardless of the flowers he crushed underfoot. He took hold of her arms so tightly that she winced, and for a second he looked as if he was about to make some angry retort, but then he recovered himself and let her go. Stepping back, he ran his hand through his dark hair.

'I'm sorry. I keep forgetting how absurdly young you are.'

But his apology did nothing to placate her. 'That's right, blame everything on my youth. Older people always do that when they're too set in their ways to bridge the generation gap. But I'll have you know that I'm twenty-two, and I'm quite old enough to make my own decisions *and* stick to them,' she emphasised.

'Good, I'm glad to hear it.' He had himself fully under control now and she could read nothing from his expression. 'If you've seen enough, perhaps we'd better go back.'

Silently Kirsty turned to follow him, but when they emerged from the wood she took careful note of where the path started so that she would be able to find it again. It would give her much pleasure to come here again alone and not have it spoiled by Gyles Grantham's disturbing presence.

His horse was still grazing quietly nearby and he sprang lightly into the saddle. Reaching down a hand, he said, 'I'll give you a lift back to your cottage.'

Kirsty hung back. 'But I can't ride.'

He looked amused. 'You don't have to do anything —just sit in the saddle.'

'But will the animal be able to carry us both?'

Gyles ran his eyes over her slim figure consideringly. 'How much do you weigh?'

She began to tell him and then realised that she was being teased.

He laughed. 'Put your right foot on mine.' She did so and he hoisted her easily up so that she was sitting side-saddle in front of him. And it wasn't until he settled himself more comfortably and put his arms round her to pick up the reins that she realised just how close to him she was, her shoulder leaning against his chest, her face very near to his. His proximity unnerved her and for a while she tried to hold herself rigidly upright so that she wasn't touching him, but she found that well-nigh impossible on horseback and had to loosen her body as they began to make their way downhill. All the same, she felt nervous and on edge. Heavens, who wouldn't when held so close to a virtual stranger, and someone she'd been having a recent feud with at that! If Gyles noticed her tension he gave no sign, talking casually to her as he pointed out various landmarks—the spire of a distant church, the highest hill in the county—until gradually she began to relax a little and to answer him.

Looking back at the hill they had just left, she said, 'It seems odd that that small wood should have been left there right at the top of the hill instead of being cleared with the rest of the land.'

'It wasn't. That land was never forested. The wood was deliberately planted there in the eighteenth century.' Seeing her look of puzzlement, Gyles explained, 'This is hunting country. But unfortunately there aren't many places where foxes can breed, so the local landowners would plant those copses especially for the foxes, and they sited them on the tops of hills so that they acted as a landmark. There are a great many of them in the country if you look.'

'I've never heard of that before. You must know a great deal about the countryside.'

'I've lived here all my life; it's my home and my livelihood.' He looked down at her and his breath brushed her hair. 'And now it's yours.'

She was saved from answering because they'd come to a gate leading into the lower meadow and he had to lean down to open it. They continued on, the horse picking its way slowly across the open field to another gate into the lane. Gyles shut it carefully behind them and went to ride up the lane to the cottage, but Kirsty said quickly. 'I can walk from here, thanks.'

'It's no trouble to take you the rest of the way.'

'No, I'd rather walk.'

He looked at her quizzically. 'Afraid of what the

neighbours might say?' But he reined in the horse and dismounted, then reached up to help her down. Putting his hands round her waist, he lifted her easily to the ground, but didn't let her go at once. 'By the way, I've instructed the staff at the garden centre to serve you with whatever you need, and as you're in business you'll be able to have everything at trade prices.'

The casual way he announced his complete change of attitude took Kirsty's breath away. Her eyes filled with bright sparks of indignation. 'And I suppose you expect me to be terribly grateful to you for your condescension. Well, I'm not. I'd rather drive fifty miles than buy anything from you!'

She tried to push him aside, but found herself between him and the horse and unable to move away. His hands tightened on her waist and she realised that her efforts to break free were completely ineffective. It was like trying to break an iron bar. Deliberately he waited until she'd stopped struggling and was glaring up at him resentfully.

Brusquely he said, 'I thought you'd agreed to call a halt to this childish behaviour. You're a businesswoman now, Kirsty, and you'll need all the advantages you can get. So for your sister's sake, if not for your own, you've got to accept my offer.'

Kirsty's resentment deepened. 'You don't pull your punches, do you? All right, maybe I have no choice—but just don't do me any favours, Mr Grantham!' Pulling free from him at last, she ducked under his arm and ran along the lane, leaving him standing looking after her, his expression unreadable.

Penny was still sitting in the garden reading a book when she got back, and looked at her flushed face curiously. 'You must have been hurrying—or have you been sunbathing?'

Kirsty forced herself to simmer down and speak lightly. 'A bit of both, I suppose. Have you had a good rest?'

'Mm, lovely. Did you meet anyone?'

'What do you mean?' Kirsty's voice was sharp.

Penny looked at her in surprise. 'Why, nothing. I just wondered if you ran into anyone on your walk, that's all.'

Turning hurriedly to go inside, Kirsty said, 'No, I didn't. No one of importance.'

But although she might deny it to Penny, Kirsty found that she couldn't dismiss Gyles Grantham from her mind so easily. All through the rest of that day her thoughts kept returning to him, no matter how hard she tried to concentrate on other things. He was older than most of the men she knew and she wasn't used to dealing with anyone who treated her so autocratically, who took it for granted that he knew what was best for her and expected her to know it too. And this very attitude aroused a stubborn streak in her that made her behave in a contrary, wilful manner, so starting the circle off again. But most disturbing of all, she found that she was now aware of him as a man and not just as her enemy. When he had held her so close to him in the saddle his nearness had affected her far more than it should have done, far more than if he had been merely someone she disliked.

As she got into bed that night and lay awake in the darkness, Kirsty realised that it was the effect he had on her which had made her want to hit out at him and to argue with him, some perverse part of her nature fighting against the attraction she felt for him. Her thoughts came to an abrupt halt. Was that what it was? Physical attraction? She must be crazy! She was in love with Simon, wasn't she? Dismissively she told herself that she was being silly, that all she really felt was simply a natural embarrassment at being held so near to a man she didn't know very well and certainly didn't trust.

The next morning Kirsty woke to the usual country sounds: Mrs Anderson's rooster crowing, the cows being rounded up in the field, the clip-clop of horses' hooves going up the lane, and birds singing their heads off outside the window. Yawningly she went to bring in the milk, happy that it was going to be another lovely day, no sign yet of April showers. She opened the front door and gazed down in surprise. Someone had left a square white box, not much smaller than a shoe-box, on the doorstep. Curiously she picked it up and carried it into the kitchen, looking to see if there was anything written on it to say who it was for or where it had come from, but it was completely blank. Carefully she removed the lid and then stared. Inside there was a large bunch of violets, the dew still on their petals, nestling against a bed of deep-green moss. Instinctively Kirsty knew who they were from even before she had picked up the card that came with them. 'Because they match your eyes, G.' And her heart gave a silly, breath-catching lurch.

CHAPTER FIVE

A COUPLE of days later the weather broke and Kirsty took advantage of the time indoors to finish the painting in the bedroom, then they took a morning off to go into town where Penny chose some pretty floral wallpaper and matching curtain material. It was rather expensive and Penny demurred at first, but Kirsty insisted that they buy it; the room was to be Penny's, and the younger girl had been so patient and uncomplaining during her illness when Kirsty had been forced to leave her alone while she got on with the garden that Kirsty felt she deserved this small treat.

Buying the wallpaper was one thing, but Kirsty found that trying to hang it on the uneven walls of the cottage was something else entirely, and she got into a hopeless mess, but luckily Dave Pagett called in one evening and came to her rescue. He had got into the habit of dropping in every now and again, mostly in the evenings, but occasionally when he wasn't busy in the morning he would walk along from the garage for a coffee. They teased him that he only came to sample Penny's delicious cakes, and he laughingly agreed, but they all knew that as soon as Penny was well enough he would ask her to go out with him.

Kirsty deliberated on whether she ought to have a quiet word with him and warn him about her sister's previous unhappy romance, but Dave seemed in no hurry to push things along, being content that they should get to know each other as friends first, and gradually Kirsty's doubts began to disappear. She real-

ised that Dave was man enough to see for himself that
Penny still sometimes withdrew into a shell and to
guess at the reason, and that he was quite capable of
handling the situation without her help. Biding his
time until he thought Penny was ready and knew him
well enough to realise that she wouldn't be hurt again.

Thinking of a possible romance for Penny inevitably led to thoughts of her own. Lately Simon had become more obdurate in his demands for her to come to
London for a weekend, but Kirsty insisted that she
couldn't yet leave Penny by herself. She was com-
pelled, though, to promise that she would as soon as
she was able. And it wasn't until some time later that
she realised that the promise had been *forced* out of
her. Although when she had moved here she had been
sure that she would miss London terribly, she now
found that she seldom gave it a thought; there was so
much to do to the cottage and garden that her every
waking moment was filled, and she had learnt to live
without the shops and entertainments when she could
look out of her window every morning to see the trees
bursting into leaf and watch her plants pushing their
way through the earth. A sort of exhilaration filled her
as she saw the garden gradually taking shape while she
used the bricks from the chimney to lay patterned
paths and pulled the weeds out of the front beds to
give the flowers a chance to grow. It was hard work,
but she felt well, and happier than she had ever expected to be.

And Simon? Did she miss him? When she pondered
that question she found that she just didn't know the
answer. Certainly she looked forward to talking to
him on the phone and would have been pleased if he'd
come down to visit them, but she knew that she was
far more reluctant to consider giving up the cottage,

not only for Penny's sake, but for her own. And when
Simon finally forced her to make a choice, she had no
idea which it would be.

As soon as the weather cleared Kirsty made a start on
cutting the inside of the front hedge, piling the clippings on the already large stack in the back garden that
she really would have to burn as soon as it dried out.
She saw several people she knew as they went past on
their way into town, and once Gyles drove by in a
silver-grey Rolls-Royce instead of his usual Range-
Rover. He saw her and waved but didn't stop, and
Kirsty found herself fighting down a feeling of disappointment. She told herself it was only because she
had wanted to thank him for the violets and wondered
why he had bothered to send them at all if he didn't
intend to follow them up. Perhaps, she conjectured, he
now regretted what was probably an impulsive action.
But somehow she thought that Gyles would never do
anything without a reason.

But any disappointment she might have felt disappeared completely the next morning. The door
knocker thundered very early while they were still
having breakfast, and when she went to open it Kirsty
found Gyles standing on the doorstep. She started to
say good morning, but one glance at the harsh, angry
look on his face and the words died in her throat.

'I want a word with you,' he said grimly, and catching hold of her arm pulled her out of the doorway and
began to march her down the path.

'What is it? What's the matter?' She tried to twist
round to face him, but he propelled her out of the garden and pushed her into his Range-Rover which was
waiting outside. Getting in beside her, he started the
engine and drove fast up the lane, his face a grim
mask.

'Will you please tell me what's going on?' Then as he still sat and ignored her, Kirsty began to get angry. 'Look, you have no right to just drag me into your car like this without a word! If you don't. . . .'

But Gyles turned to her, his eyes furious. 'Shut up! If you don't want me to lose my temper completely, then just keep quiet.'

Kirsty stared at him, frightened by the depth of his anger and wondering what on earth she'd done to arouse it. She soon found out. He turned out of the lane and into a long single-track driveway with the name Manor Farm on a signboard, and pulled up in a large farmyard. But he hardly even gave her time to look round before he had yanked her out of the vehicle and was pulling her across to a large barn. Several people were standing near a doorway at the far end and they looked at her in open curiosity, but Gyles ignored them and hurried her inside. She found herself in a section of the barn partitioned off from the main part; it had been painted white and there was fresh, clean straw on the floor. The place smelt of antiseptic and reminded her vaguely of a hospital. There were four or five men already there and two of them, who wore white coats, were on their knees and working on a Jersey cow which lay on the straw and was obviously in pain, judging from the terrible noises that the poor creature made. All the men turned towards her as Gyles pulled her in and Kirsty recoiled at the contempt and disgust in the looks they gave her. One of them even deliberately turned his back on her. She knew then that something was wrong, appallingly wrong, and that concerned her. But how?

She turned to Gyles in frightened bewilderment. 'I —I don't understand. Why have you brought me here?'

For answer he led her out of the barn and towards a field entrance. Kirsty went with him willingly enough, she couldn't stand having those men looking at her like that another minute. He held open the gate for her and she preceded him into the field, but stopped dead when she saw the carcases of some more cows lying on the grass. She went to turn away, but Gyles caught hold of her shoulders and forced her to turn back. His voice was harsh in her ear.

'Look at them, Kirsty. Take a good look. See what your thoughtlessness has led to. These animals have died because of your stupidity and we'll be lucky if the vet can save the other. Prize cattle that have taken years of careful breeding to produce—and you've killed them in a day!' His voice filled with disgust and his fingers bit cruelly into her shoulders. 'Go on—take a closer look at your handiwork.'

He let her go suddenly, pushing her towards the dead animals so that Kirsty almost lost her balance. She turned to him, her face pale. 'But I haven't done anything to them. I haven't been near them. You're making a mistake.'

'It's no mistake. Look.' He strode to a sack that was lying on the ground near the cows and upturned it. A pile of twigs and leaves fell out at his feet and Kirsty realised dazedly that they were clippings from her front hedge. She stared at them in bewilderment.

'But I don't understand. What have they got to do with the cows?'

Gyles looked at her impatiently. 'It's yew, Kirsty. It's poisonous to farm animals. God, you're so ignorant you probably didn't even know what it was.'

Kirsty looked at him unhappily. 'Yes, I did—someone told me. But I don't understand how they got it. How could they get in the garden?'

His look turned to one of anger. 'They didn't have to. Because you were too lazy to clear up your own rubbish and threw it over into the field! The men found it there at the back of your garden this morning.'

Her face suddenly ashen, Kirsty gazed at him in appalled dismay. 'But that isn't true! I didn't. I piled all the rubbish in the back garden ready to burn.'

The harsh look in his eyes turned to contempt. 'Don't try to lie your way out of it, Kirsty. I know that you're still ignorant of country ways and if you'd come right out and apologised for what you'd done I'd have been more than willing to forgive and forget. But to try and wriggle out of responsibility with a brazen lie!'

'It's not a lie,' Kirsty said vehemently. 'I tell you I didn't throw the cuttings over.'

'No?' His voice was openly sneering. 'Then who did?'

She shrugged helplessly. 'I don't know. But I swear it wasn't me.' She saw the look of scornful disbelief on his face and impulsively stepped towards him, putting a hand on his arm. 'Please, Gyles, you've got to believe me,' she said desperately.

Deliberately he looked down at her hand and shook it off as if it was something dirty. Starting to shake with emotion, Kirsty gazed helplessly into his set face, then turned with a sob and began to run across the field, away from the contempt in his eyes.

She didn't stop running until she reached the gate leading into her own back garden, and then she leaned against it, panting for breath and with the tears still running down her face. How could he be so cruel, so unjust? Her hands were trembling and she gripped the top bar of the gate hard to try and stop them. She was horrified by what had happened and could still hear the noise made by the poor sick cow ringing through her head, but what had shaken her most was the way in which the men had looked at her and the withering contempt in Gyles' eyes when she had protested her innocence. And of course he hadn't believed her; he had merely despised her even more, thinking her a liar as well as a thoughtless idiot. And it had hurt, that look—she felt shrivelled up inside.

'Kirsty! Kirsty, what is it?' Penny came running across the garden towards her, her face frightened and anxious. 'What did he do to you?'

Trying to pull herself together for Penny's sake, Kirsty wiped her eyes and climbed over the gate into the garden. 'It was a mistake. Nothing to do with us, after all,' she answered, trying to keep her voice light.

'So why are you crying?' Penny squared her shoulders. 'Kirsty, will you please stop trying to shield me and tell me what's happened,' she said forcefully.

So Kirsty told her; after all, it would probably rebound on Penny as much as her. When she had finished the younger girl stared at her aghast. 'He thinks you did it deliberately?'

Kirsty shook her head. 'No, he thought I was just lazy and ignorant, and it wasn't until I told him that it wasn't me that he really got nasty.' The memory of it made her shiver again.

'But I don't understand,' said Penny, walking towards the pile of garden rubbish. 'It's yards from the gate. The clippings couldn't have blown over, could they?'

Kirsty joined her and shook her head. 'There wasn't any wind yesterday, and if there had been the stuff would be all over the garden.'

'Well, if you didn't do it, there can only be one solution.' Penny looked at her unhappily. 'Someone must have got into the garden and deliberately taken some clippings and put them into the field, knowing that it would poison the cows.'

'I know,' Kirsty admitted reluctantly. 'And whoever it was must have been a country person to know that yew was poisonous. Somebody must want us out of here pretty badly,' she added miserably.

'Well, we both know who that is,' Penny pointed out vehemently. 'The Squire!'

Kirsty turned to her with a shocked face. 'But it couldn't possibly be him. He wouldn't deliberately poison prize animals.'

'Why not? They're not his cows, are they? They belong to the farm. And he's already done his best to try and get rid of us, so what makes you think he wouldn't go this far?'

'But I told you; when he found out there were just the two of us he said he wanted to help us. And he said we could get whatever we wanted from his garden centre.'

Penny snorted. 'Oh, that's really big of him—especially now that we've proved that we can get along without it.'

Kirsty stared at her sister incredulously. 'But he was so angry, really furious. No one could have pretended that kind of feeling.'

'You don't know him well enough to say that. He's probably quite capable of putting on any act he likes. I wouldn't be surprised if he isn't telling everyone right now how he offered us friendship and help, and now we've done this to the farmer. You realise that after this none of the villagers will want to have anything to do with us,' she said bitterly.

Quickly Kirsty crossed to her. 'Yes, they will. Because we'll tell them the truth. They're not all influenced by the Squire, you know. And if you think a thing like this will keep Dave away, you're very much mistaken. A whole herd of dead cows wouldn't keep him away from your cooking,' she added in a sorry attempt to cheer the younger girl up.

But Penny couldn't even manage a smile. 'It would be a whole lot better if we could prove it wasn't us.'

Kirsty nodded and looked glumly at the muddy ground. 'We'd better go inside, your feet will get cold in the mud.'

Penny obediently went to go in, leaving a trail of footsteps behind her, and Kirsty moved to follow but suddenly stopped dead. 'Penny! If whoever it was took the clippings last night, they must have walked across this mud. If we can find a footprint....'

Frenziedly she looked round at the ground and Penny hurried to join her.

'There must be something. Look, over there.' She pointed excitedly to part of a heelmark on the very edge of a clump of grass a few feet from the bonfire. 'It's much larger than our heelmarks. It must have been made by a man in gumboots.'

'But it's so far from the pile,' Penny objected. 'No one could possibly have taken a stride that long.'

'No, not unless he realised that the ground was muddy and put something down to tread on and hide his steps.' Kirsty searched round between the mark and the bonfire. 'Yes, look. You can just see the outline where a piece of cardboard or wood has been laid on the ground, but unfortunately we've walked right over it and almost obscured it. If only we'd thought to look first,' she said hopelessly. 'No one will ever believe us just from this.'

'The police might.'

Kirsty stared at her aghast. 'The police? We can't go to them.'

'Why not? We're going to need all the help we can get to fight the Squire.'

'Penny, we can't be sure it was him. It could have been anyone. And I still don't believe that he'd do this to us,' Kirsty added emphatically, although her mind was a turmoil of doubt and uncertainty.

She insisted that Penny go in while she poured paraffin over the bonfire and set light to it, making sure that every twig and leaf was burned, that there would be nothing left for anyone to play the same trick on them again. For the rest of the day she tried to concentrate on her work, but all the time she was turning the thing over and over in her mind, wondering whether Penny was right and she should have called in the police. After all, she'd been accused of a crime she hadn't committed and she had the right to try to clear her name. But somehow she shrank from taking the matter further. There would be lots of questions and she would have to say if she suspected anyone and then it would all come out. She could imagine the look that would come into Gyles' face at her accusation, and all her senses shrank from such a confrontation. But more than anything she couldn't believe that he could be so two-faced, to offer friendship one day and to do this to them the next. No, it was impossible.

Her mind also went to the farmer who owned the cattle; she had no idea of the value of the animals but guessed they must have been worth quite a lot of money. The thought that the man had suffered this loss because of some cruel trick played against her haunted her and added to her worries and anxieties. It was so unfair on him when he was just an innocent bystander. She could guess how much he must despise her and felt sick with worry at having made such an enemy, especially knowing that however much she proclaimed her innocence no one was going to believe her.

After a long, sleepless night of mental stress, Kirsty made up her mind that she couldn't possibly let the farmer suffer. She would have to offer to pay for the cows. If this made her look guilty she couldn't help it. There was no other way of avoiding turning the farmer and possibly the whole village against them. Deciding that if the thing was to be done it had better be done straight away, Kirsty dressed in a tweed skirt and jacket and put on some make-up; she would need to feel as confident as possible in her coming interview with the farmer. She was much too tense and nervous to eat breakfast and couldn't settle to any housework while she waited until she judged it would be all right to call at the farm. Luckily Penny was still in bed; Kirsty didn't want to worry the younger girl with this until it was over. Right or wrong, she felt it was the only thing to do.

At exactly nine o'clock she set off up the lane, taking a big gulp before she turned into the driveway leading to the farm and an even bigger one before she raised a shaking hand to knock at the door. It was opened by a buxom woman in a floral apron who, Kirsty remembered, had been standing outside the barn the previous day. The woman looked at her in astonishment.

'What do *you* want?'

Kirsty flushed at her tone and said hurriedly, 'Please, I'd like to speak to the farmer. I'm sorry, I don't know his name.'

His name's Ted Singleton. And I'm Mrs Singleton,' the woman said coldly. 'What do you want with him?'

'I-it's a personal matter,' Kirsty faltered unhappily, aware of the woman's scornful gaze.

'Is it now? Well, you won't find him here. He's gone up to the Manor.'

'Oh. Will he be long, do you think?'

Mrs Singleton shrugged. 'All morning, I shouldn't wonder. There's a lot to sort out after yesterday,' she added meaningfully.

Kirsty wilted for a moment, but then the knowledge that she was completely innocent helped her and she squared her shoulders and faced up to the farmer's wife. 'Thank you,' she said firmly. 'I'll look for him there, then.' And she managed to walk steadily across the yard although the woman's eyes were burning holes in her back. Probably making sure I don't contaminate her pigs, or something, she thought resentfully. It was so *unfair*!

Grimly she walked back to the lane and continued up it until she came to an imposing gateway between two tall brick pillars with a small, discreet sign announcing that this was Notley Manor. The drive was wide and had large clumps of rhododendron bushes among the trees on either side which she guessed would look beautiful when they were in bloom in a couple of months' time, but right now she was too busy worrying about how she could get hold of Mr Singleton without seeing Gyles as well to notice her surroundings. But when she turned a bend in the driveway and saw the Manor house before her she had to give it her full attention.

It was a beautiful place, built on two storeys with arched windows whose latticed diamond leads caught the sun and gave it a welcoming appearance, and with the tall, ornate chimneys that only Tudor buildings have. Her feet crunched on the thick, well-weeded

gravel of the drive and as she came nearer she wondered for a moment whether she ought perhaps to find
the tradesmen's entrance, but then she resolutely
walked up to the front door. If she was going to beard
the lion in his den she would do it without sneaking
round to the back entrance. There was a big iron
handle that she pulled and the door was quickly
opened by an elderly butler.

'Good morning. I'm trying to find Mr Singleton. I
was told that he was here.'

The man motioned her inside. 'Your name, miss?'

'Miss Naylor.'

He asked her to wait and Kirsty was able to look
around her. The main door opened straight into a
great hall, very high and with panelled walls which
were lined with paintings, landscapes mostly. The floor
was of polished wood enriched with one or two rugs
and the furniture was mostly antique; heavy leather
chairs, a buttoned settee and a big refectory table with
a huge copper bowl full of daffodils on it. At the far
end there was a wide flight of stairs, still of uncarpeted
polished wood, mounting to a gallery that ran along
the length of the room.

The butler came back and said, 'If you would follow
me, please, Miss Naylor.'

He led the way through a door at one end and down
a corridor. Kirsty could feel her heart hammering in
her chest and just hoped that Mr Singleton would be
alone. But as they neared the double doors at the end
of the corridor, the butler said, 'I'm afraid that both
Mr Singleton and Mr Grantham have gone into Barham, but if you will wait in here, Mrs Grantham will
be down in a moment.'

'Oh, but I . . . .' But before she could find words to
tell him she'd rather not wait, the man had gone and

left her alone in a pleasant morning-room that over-
looked the landscaped gardens at the back of the
house. Kirsty stood in perplexed indecision. He had
said *Mrs* Grantham. It had never occurred to her that
Gyles might be married. No one had ever mentioned
his wife—and Kirsty found that she had no wish to
meet her. But she couldn't just walk out. Pacing restlessly up and down the room she wondered what to
do, then made up her mind; she had come to see Mr
Singleton and if he wasn't here there was no point in
staying. She took a couple of determined steps towards the doors, but then the butler pushed them
open and stood aside to let a woman enter. But she
didn't walk in; she steered herself in an electrically-
driven wheelchair. And she was middle-aged, in her
mid-fifties, Kirsty judged, her grey hair drawn back
in a bun. She propelled the wheelchair to a space on
one side of the fire that crackled in the big old hearth
and waited until the butler had arranged a rug around
her knees and withdrawn before she spoke.

'Good morning. I'm sorry my son isn't here, but perhaps I can help you.'

'Well, no, I'm afraid not. You see it wasn't really
Mr Grantham that I wanted to see. I wanted to talk
to Mr Singleton.'

'He was here earlier, but they've gone into Barham
and probably won't be back until after lunch. It's the
cattle market today, you know.'

'In that case I'll call on him at his farm this evening. I just wanted to see him about some cows he
owns.'

'But Mr Singleton doesn't own any cattle. The farm
belongs to my son. Mr Singleton is only the farm manager.'

'Oh, I see.' Kirsty felt at a loss. 'Well, I'm sorry to

have disturbed you.' She turned to go, but the other woman stopped her.

'Please don't rush away. Parker will be bringing coffee directly. Won't you sit down and join me?' And she gave Kirsty such a warm smile that she felt bemused and automatically sat down in a comfortable armchair on the other side of the fireplace. 'You've taken over Briar Cottage, haven't you? I believe Gyles mentioned it.'

Kirsty looked at her rather suspiciously, imagining just what Gyles had said about her, but Mrs Grantham's face gave nothing away, she merely looked politely enquiring, and Kirsty decided that Gyles probably kept anything of an upsetting nature from her. 'Yes, we moved in last month.'

'I think it's quite old, almost as old as this house. And I've an idea it once belonged to the estate,' Mrs Grantham remarked. 'I believe it was originally used as a house for retired servants, but then one of the previous Granthams found it a convenient place to keep his mistress in—however, his wife found out and made him sell it.'

Kirsty's eyes flew wide in surprise at this unexpected piece of information and Mrs Grantham smiled. 'I thought that would surprise you.'

The butler came in with the coffee tray then and placed it on a small table at her hostess' elbow. He served Kirsty and quietly went away again.

'If you're interested in the history of your house I'd be glad to look up the records for you.'

Kirsty smiled. 'Thank you, I'd like that very much. We found an inglenook fireplace in the sitting-room, but unfortunately we haven't had time to do anything other than expose it yet.'

They went on chatting and soon Kirsty felt completely at ease with Mrs Grantham, who seemed interested in everything she had to say. She was still a very good-looking woman and must have been beautiful when she was younger, but although she was neatly dressed, she wore no make-up and seemed not to care much about her appearance other than to be tidy and clean. She was talking animatedly enough now, but Kirsty guessed that this was only a temporary thing and that when she was alone she was unhappy and depressed, only rousing herself for visitors. She had seen too many people like it when she worked at the hospital not to recognise the symptoms, and she had voluntarily given up many of her evenings to sit and talk with the patients in an effort to encourage them to hope, to convince them that life had still much to offer them.

Impulsively she leaned forward. 'Perhaps you'd like to come and visit us at the cottage? I'd enjoy showing you what we intend to do with the garden.'

Mrs Grantham smiled, but Kirsty could almost sense her withdrawing into herself. 'That's very kind of you, my dear, but I haven't left the house for quite some time now.' With an expressive gesture of her hand she indicated the wheelchair.

Kirsty looked at her sadly. 'You've given up.' It was a statement, not a question.

For a moment the older woman's chin came up and she recognised the cool, autocratic look she had seen on Gyles' face, but then Mrs Grantham suddenly sagged in her chair, her face lined with unhappiness. 'Oh, dear, does it show so much?'

Kirsty crossed swiftly to kneel down beside her and take her hand, trying to pass some of her young strength through her touch. 'Only to me. You put on a wonderful act, but I've worked in a hospital and I've met many people who were going through what you're going through at the moment. They think there's nothing left for them and wish that they had been killed rather than maimed. I've seen young men in their twenties who've been in car accidents and who've begged the doctors to put them down like a dog, but later they've realised that half a life is better than no life at all and before long they're dancing with their girl-friends in their wheelchairs.'

Mrs Grantham gave a wan smile. 'I know you're trying to be kind, child, but I've been crippled for a long time. I had a riding accident when Gyles was only a boy. The bones didn't knit together properly and I've never walked since. Oh, at first I accepted it because there was always the hope that one day I would be cured. But now so many years have gone by.' She gave a little hopeless shrug.

'So you've let yourself get defeated and just gradually withdrawn until you don't go outside the house any more, and soon you won't go outside your bedroom and then you'll stay in bed like an invalid until you let yourself die.' Deliberately Kirsty sounded rather scornful. 'And you'll be too tired to let your friends come and visit you, and you'll allow your relations to worry themselves sick because you won't tell them the truth and let them help you. Why, I bet you even put on this act that there's nothing wrong to your own son!'

Mrs Grantham stared at Kirsty, her eyes wide and shocked. 'I pretend to him most of all.' She gripped Kirsty's hand tightly. 'Will—will it really be like that?'

'Yes, it will.' She paused a moment to let it sink in, then said urgently, 'Unless you realise now, before it's too late, that you owe it to the people who love you to try and snap out of it and start living again.'

'But—but it's been so long. I don't know how.'

Kirsty stood up. 'It's really very simple. We'll start right now. Is this your shawl?' She took the shawl from a nearby chair and draped it over the elderly woman's shoulders, then pushed open some casement doors leading out into the garden and saw that a ramp had been built over the steps. Turning back to Mrs Grantham she said, 'It's a lovely day. Won't you make it the first day of your future?'

She waited, knowing that the impetus must come from Mrs Grantham herself. Slowly the woman guided her chair to the doorway and then hesitated. Kirsty held out a hand towards her. She took it and held it tightly. And then she was down the ramp and outside, both of them laughing a little with relief.

Kirsty didn't let her stay out too long. Just ten minutes in which they wandered round the garden and Kirsty picked flowers and put them in the older woman's hands. After she'd helped her back inside she took her leave, confident that once started, Mrs Grantham would find the courage to go on. She thought about it as she walked home and it wasn't until she had almost reached the end of the lane that she realised that it was Gyles himself who owned the dead cows and that he couldn't possibly have deliberately poisoned his own cattle. And strangely enough this knowledge made her worries feel a whole lot lighter and she was humming happily to herself as she turned into the cottage.

CHAPTER SIX

KIRSTY'S visit to the Manor had unexpected results, for later that day Penny went to answer a knock at the door and ushered in an elderly man who introduced himself as Mr Reynolds.

'Mrs Grantham is an old friend of mine,' he explained. 'I teach history at the college in Barham and I'm also the secretary of the Local History Society. Mrs Grantham phoned me this morning to tell me about the inglenook you found here, and I wondered if I might have a look at it?'

'Why, of course.' Kirsty led the way into the sitting-room. 'I'm afraid all we've done is pull out the old Victorian fireplace. We haven't had time to do anything more.'

Mr Reynolds examined the inglenook minutely. 'It's a very good example. And the rest of the room looks interesting too. If you take down that plasterboard on the ceiling you'll probably find the original beams underneath. Do you know much about restoring old property?'

'Not a thing,' Kirsty confessed. 'We'll just have to get some books from the library and find out as we go.'

Their visitor looked at them thoughtfully before accepting Penny's offer of a cup of tea. Over it he told them about some of the projects the Society had undertaken.

'I wonder,' he said rather diffidently, 'if you would consider letting the Society undertake the restoration of your sitting-room? We have several very keen members who could come along in their spare time and work on it.'

'That's very kind of you, Mr Reynolds. Ordinarily I would have jumped at the offer, but unfortunately we just can't afford to pay anyone to do the work,' Kirsty admitted honestly. 'But, thanks, anyway.'

'Oh, you won't have to pay them. They would be pleased to do it for the experience and the pleasure that they'd get out of it. Although we would want to take photographs of the progress as we went along, if you wouldn't mind?'

'Mind? Good heavens, no. Why, that's wonderful. We'd be terribly grateful.'

'That's settled, then,' Mr Reynolds smiled. 'It's May Day next week, so I suggest we start then if it's convenient.'

The sisters assured him that it was and hugged each other gleefully when he'd gone.

'I must write to Mrs Grantham and thank her,' Kirsty exclaimed.

'Why don't you go and see her again?' Penny enquired. 'You seemed to get on all right with her this morning.'

Kirsty shook her head. 'No, I've given her the little push she needed, but now the rest must come from her. If I go to see her again she might rely on me instead of herself. I'll just write a note and take it up to the letterbox at the gates of the Manor.'

But there were household chores to do first and it was dark again before Kirsty set out on her errand. A slight breeze had blown the clouds away and the night was clear and bright, the stars shining like tiny diamonds strewn across the sky. The wind ruffled the leaves in the trees and from one of them a nightjar flew out as she passed, startling her with its harsh cry. There were other noises from the nocturnal creatures in the hedgerows, and once a rabbit scuttled across the lane towards the meadow, its white bobtail clear in the moonlight.

Kirsty quickened her pace as she neared the Manor gates, her footsteps echoing along the metalled road in the darkness, but then, seemingly from nowhere, a voice said sharply, 'Who's there?' and she almost jumped out of her skin.

A man came out of the gateway and to her consternation she saw that it was Gyles. He crossed quickly towards her and she stifled an urge to turn and run. Their confrontation the previous day was still too raw for her to face him again with any equanimity.

'Kirsty?'

'Yes.'

He came nearer so that he could see her clearly. 'Out for a walk?'

'No. I—I came to deliver a letter.' She lifted her hand to show him the envelope in it.

'For me?'

'No, for your mother.'

'Ah, yes. She told me you called earlier. I'll take it for her, shall I?'

Kirsty held it out to him and found to her annoyance that her hand was shaking.

He put it in his pocket. 'My mother said you wanted to see Ted Singleton about the cows?'

He was very close and Kirsty glanced quickly up at him. The moonlight accentuated the angles of his face and gave his lean features an almost satanic appearance. Instinctively she moved a little away from him. His lips hardened into a thin line.

'Yes, I thought they were his. I didn't realise the farm belonged to you.'

'Manor Farm has always been run by a manager and supplies the house, but the other farms on the estate are run by tenant farmers who own their livestock, so it was a natural mistake.' He waited but when she didn't go on he asked, 'What did you want to say about the cows?'

Kirsty put her hands in the pockets of her jacket and turned away, walking a few paces from him before she spoke. 'I—I wanted to offer to pay for them,' she said, her eyes fixed on the ground.

'You admit you were responsible, then?'

She turned to find him watching her intently. She opened her mouth to deny it, but then shrugged mentally. What was the use? He would never believe her. 'The hedge clippings were from my garden, yes.'

His voice hardened. 'Why didn't you admit it at the time? No one thought that you'd done it deliberately and it would have saved a great deal of bad feeling if you'd. . . .'

'Will you please stop lecturing me?' Kirsty broke in sharply. 'If you'll just tell me how much the animals were worth, I'll send you a cheque first thing in the morning.'

Gyles stepped angrily towards her. 'Do you know the value of prize cattle?'

'No, but it doesn't matter how much they cost because I'll raise a loan against the house if I have to. Just tell me how much!' Her voice started to rise hysterically. 'I'd rather sell the place than be indebted to you!'

'You stubborn little fool!' Kirsty tried to turn away, but he caught her arms and jerked her angrily round to face him. 'Do you really think all I care about is their value? It's the waste of their lives that angers me. That, and the progeny we hoped to have bred from them. All right, the animals were insured, but money can't replace the years of work that went into breeding them.' He stared intently into her face, but she kept her eyes firmly lowered and his voice hardened again. 'But I don't suppose you've taken in a word I've said. You're like all townspeople—you think that writing out a cheque solves everything, puts everything right again. Well, it doesn't, not here. And now you'll have lost the respect of the whole village, just because you were too much of a coward to tell the truth earlier.'

When she still stayed silent he shook her roughly. 'Do you understand what I'm saying to you? Do you?' he demanded angrily.

Enraged beyond words, Kirsty put up her hands and tried vainly to push him away, and when she couldn't balled her hands up into fists and beat furiously against his chest. 'Let go of me, damn you! How dare you speak to me like. . . .'

'You little spitfire!' Gyles jerked her towards him, imprisoning her arms against his chest.

For a few moments Kirsty continued to struggle, but suddenly became aware of the hardness of his body against her own, of his arms like steel bands holding her pressed close to him and of his face just a few inches away, of the sheer animal maleness of him. She became very still, her pulses racing, her mind in a whirl and yet all her senses throbbing with awareness. His breathing sounded uneven in her ears and she suddenly realised that he was as conscious of their closeness as she. But he didn't let her go, instead his arms tightened and he looked down at her with a strange glint in his dark eyes. Her heart came up into her throat and a wave of heat seemed to set her insides on fire. Slowly he bent his head towards her.

Blind panic filled her and she turned her head

sharply away. 'Let me go!' she gasped. And then on a
rising note of alarm, 'Let me go. You're hurting me!'

Immediately he released her and took a step backwards. 'I'm sorry,' he bit out abruptly, and dug his
hands into his pockets. 'I didn't mean to hurt you.'

Kirsty stared at him, fists clenched, her voice unsteady. 'No, you'd draw the line at that, wouldn't you?
It wouldn't be the gentlemanly thing to do to hurt a
woman physically, but it doesn't matter how much
you hurt me mentally by accusing me of being a fool
and a liar, let alone all the things you thought me
when we first moved here.'

His voice was harsh. 'What else am I supposed to
think when you deny your guilt one day and then
admit it the next?'

'I didn't admit anything. I just said that I felt responsible because the clippings came from my garden.'
She looked at him pleadingly. 'You jumped to con-
clusions and were wrong about us before, can't you
admit that it's possible you've been mistaken this
time?'

He looked at her for a long moment, his face brood-
ing, then he gave an abrupt, negative shake of his head.
'I want to, Kirsty, but there's no other possible ex-
planation and I....'

But Kirsty didn't wait to hear him finish. 'Oh, what
does it matter? What the hell do I care what you think
of me?' And she turned with a sob that belied her
words and ran down the lane towards the cottage.

That weekend the members of the Local History
Society arrived early on the Saturday morning and were
soon hard at work. They were a friendly crowd of a
mixed age group and there was a lot of laughter and
frequent breaks for liquid refreshment to wash down

the cakes and scones that Penny pressed on them. The two girls felt duty bound to be on hand in case the workers needed anything, but on the Monday the work had progressed so well that they took the afternoon off and walked down to the village green to watch the May festivities. Several stalls and sideshows had been set up, and after they'd watched the children weaving through the intricate maypole dances they wandered around, stopping to buy home-made fudge or guess the weight of a cake. They were trying their luck at bowling for a pig, when Dave Pagett joined them and spent the rest of the afternoon with them. Kirsty was pleased to see him, not only for his own sake, but also because she had noticed one or two people giving them curious glances and guessed that the story of the cows must have got round, so she was grateful to him for the support his presence gave them.

While they were watching the tug-of-war beween a team from the local pub and those from surrounding villages, Kirsty turned and under cover of the enthusiastic shouts of encouragement, asked him whether he had heard.

He nodded. 'One of Ted Singleton's farm hands was talking about it in the pub the day it happened, although apparently the Squire had told them not to say anything. But this chap told it in confidence to some-one and was overheard; purposely, I shouldn't wonder, and it was all over the village in no time.'

'I see.' Kirsty looked at him in some dismay.

'Shouldn't worry about it too much, though,' Dave said reassuringly. 'Nobody blames you; things like that happen all the time in the country.'

'But they think I lied about it, don't they?' she said bitterly.

'They just think the Squire frightened the wits out

of you.' He gave a chuckle. 'This chap said he hadn't
seen the Squire so mad in years!'

Kirsty derived a little comfort from his words and was
able to watch the displays of Morris dancing and the
comedy of Saint George and the Dragon that followed
without her mind being so clouded with anxiety. She
found that she very much wanted to be a part of the
crowd of spectators, all of whom knew one another and
knew the players as well, so that every line was greeted
with ribald comments and witticisms that made the
villagers roar with laughter but meant nothing to out-
siders. Dave tried to explain, but got so involved with
village histories that he eventually gave up.

There was to be a dance in the village hall that evening and Dave asked them both to go, but Kirsty tact-
fully said that she must stay at the cottage while insist-
ing that Penny go instead.

'But don't let her overdo it,' she warned Dave when
he called to collect Penny and was waiting for her to
get ready. 'She still gets tired very easily.'

Perhaps Kirsty did feel a little wistful as she watched
them set off, Penny flushed and excited, Dave with his
hand under her elbow in a proprietorial mixture of
pride and care, but she determinedly pushed it aside;
now was no time to start feeling lonely or maudlin.
And when Mr Reynolds called her in to look at the
finished room, she was glad she'd stayed. The members
of the Society stood aside as she walked in and watched
for her reaction with eager expectancy. Kirsty stood
in the middle of the room and just stared, open-
mouthed, at the transformation.

'Why—why, it's fantastic!' And in fact she hardly
recognised the place as being the same shabby room.
They had stripped off the old plaster from walls and
ceilings to expose the original beams, and these they

had cleaned and treated to bring out the colour and age of the wood. Then they had carefully re-plastered in between the beams, making the room look far larger than it had before. The brickwork of the ingle-nook had been cleaned with a wire brush and shone its original deep red colour which looked warm and attractive even without a fire, and the carving on the thick oak lintel could be clearly seen as a design of swathes of vine leaves and bunches of grapes. On top of all this they had mended the broken panes in the lat-ticed windows and repainted all the woodwork and the window-seat. They had even cleaned the floor and varnished it.

'There are still one or two things we have to do, of course,' Mr Reynolds told her. 'We still have to emul-sion the walls and ceiling when the new plaster dries out, but we should be able to do that in a couple of days and then you can use the room.'

'It's marvellous. I'd never have believed it could look so good.' Kirsty was warm with her thanks and praise, which they seemed to appreciate. Then someone suggested that they all go for a drink, so they made their way to the village pub and took up half the space in the small saloon bar, where they sat around laugh-ing and talking until closing time.

'Have you got much furniture for the room?' Mr Reynolds asked her.

'Only a couple of armchairs and a bookcase, I'm afraid. We moved here from quite a small apartment, you see,' Kirsty explained.

'Hm. I wonder then if you'd like to come with me to a sale I'm going to later on this week? There will be a lot of stuff pulled out of old pubs when they were modernised. You might be able to pick up something quite cheaply.'

Kirsty agreed enthusiastically and he arranged to pick them up early on Wednesday morning.

So when Penny got home later that night she found Kirsty waiting up for her and poring over a list she was making. Kirsty showed her the sitting-room and then said eagerly, 'I've been going into our finances and we're not too badly off at all really. I think we could probably afford to buy a settee or something, and perhaps a sideboard. And do you think you could alter the curtains we brought from the apartment to fit these windows?'

'I don't see why not. Yes, they'd look good in here.'

'Do you think you could do it by the weekend?'

Penny looked at her elder sister in surprise. 'Why? What have you got in mind?'

'Well, I thought it would be rather nice if we gave a small party as a kind of thank-you gesture to all the people who've helped us. And I thought we could invite Mrs Anderson, because she was so kind to us when you were ill.'

Penny's eyes lit up with anticipation. 'That's a great idea. Can we invite Dave?'

Kirsty smiled inwardly. 'Of course, that goes without saying.'

'And you could invite Simon down; he's bound to be impressed when he sees how well we're getting along.'

'Mm. Look, I've made a list. It would come to about twenty people if everyone came.' She hesitated. 'There is just one other person I wanted to invite.' Penny raised her eyebrows enquiringly and Kirsty said slowly, 'It's Mrs Grantham. If it hadn't been for her the room would still be a horrible mess. And I think it would be good for her if she agreed to come.'

'But she's in a wheelchair,' Penny objected.

'Yes, I know. Which means that we can't ask her

without asking her son to bring her.'

'The Squire? You'd ask him after all he's done to us? No, I don't want to see him again!' Penny said vehemently.

'Penny, please. You've only met him once and that was under the very worst circumstances. I don't know who it was who poisoned the cows, but it certainly wasn't him; after all, he lost more by it than we did. In fact it was probably done by someone who wanted to hurt him and we were just conveniently on hand to throw the blame on.'

'Well, I can believe that,' Penny exclaimed. 'He probably has loads of enemies if he goes round accusing people as he did us.'

'But that's all over,' Kirsty said persuasively. 'He's offered us friendship and I think the least we can do is meet him halfway.'

Penny was still extremely reluctant, but by dint of a great deal of cajolery Kirsty eventually got her way, although afterwards she lay in bed and wondered just why she'd gone to such lengths. For his mother's sake, of course, she told herself sternly, so that she might be induced to leave the Manor for a while. What other reason could there possibly be?

The invitations they wrote out and despatched the next morning, but Kirsty approached the phone call to Simon with less confidence.

'This Saturday?' he said rather sharply, and Kirsty could almost imagine his frown. 'That's rather short notice. I'm afraid I've already arranged to play in a cricket match.'

'Please try, Simon. I so much want you to see the work we've done on the place and meet our new friends and neighbours.'

'No, I'm sorry, Kirsty, but I can't let my team down.

We'll have to make it some other time.' He was about to say more, but Kirsty broke across him.

'Simon.' She hesitated, and then said with a definite catch in her voice, 'Simon, I *need* you.'

There was a long pause. 'All right, I'll come. I'll be down on Saturday evening, after the match.'

And Kirsty replaced the receiver with a hand that shook despite all her efforts to control it.

There had been more than a hint of entreaty in her voice and she felt a great wave of relief when she knew that Simon was coming. She found that she needed desperately to see him again, to be reassured of her own feelings for him. And she felt confident that once she saw him all the emotions which had started to get mixed up inside her just lately would immediately sort themselves out and become straightforward again. It could only be not having seen him for so many weeks that made her feel so unsettled and on edge. In her heart she knew that the whole idea of the party had really been only an excuse so that she would have a reason for inviting Simon to come down for the weekend.

By Saturday evening Kirsty was a bag of nerves. They had gone with Mr Reynolds to the sale and had bought an old carved oak cupboard and a wooden settle which Kirsty had polished till they shone. Penny had altered the curtains and with the material left over had covered some cushions for the settle. They had also purchased a light fitting and had arranged a few ornaments and vases of flowers round the room as well as lighting a log fire in the inglenook so that the room looked warm and inviting. They had spent the whole of the morning cooking, and now the dishes of cheese straws, plates of vol-au-vents, salmon mousse, pâté, and baskets of French bread and bowls of salad were all ready. For drinks, Kirsty had made a big bowl of wine cup for the women and had got beer for the men, together with a couple of bottles of sherry.

At six-thirty she went up to have a leisurely bath and to change into her favourite dress; pale mauve and full-skirted, it had batwing sleeves and a U-shaped neckline. It was simply cut but it fitted her perfectly, emphasising her slim waist and the curve of her firm breasts. She added the kind of make-up she would normally wear for a party in London and her hair she had already blow-dried into a flicked-back style that was all the rage among her modish contemporaries. When she was ready she added scent and a gold locket that had belonged to her mother and then examined herself critically in the mirror. Not bad, considering she hadn't been near a hairdresser in weeks, and working so hard had made her lose a little weight, which helped. And she definitely looked a different person entirely than in her usual workaday outfits of jeans and sweater.

Glancing at her watch she saw that it was nearly eight, and suddenly she began to shake with nerves and her chest felt tight and constricted. She put up a trembling hand to her flushed face. What was the matter with her? It was only a party. Nothing to get so worked up about. She realised that it must be because Simon was coming and resolutely told herself that she'd be fine once he arrived. But her legs still felt like jelly when she went downstairs, and she had to force herself to smile at Penny and compliment her on the pretty print dress she was wearing.

There was nothing more to do really, but they were both excited and nervous and moved about unnecessarily straightening cushions and repositioning ashtrays, so that it came almost as a relief when the knocker sounded and the first guests arrived. They had arranged that Penny would open the door and take the coats while Kirsty introduced everyone and handed out drinks, but she was so sure that Simon would be the first to arrive that she went out into the hall with Penny. But it was Mr Reynolds, who had brought his wife along and had also given a lift to two members of the Society, and Kirsty had to hide a deep feeling of disappointment as she smilingly greeted them and ushered them into the sitting-room. They were soon followed by others, including Dave who arrived escorting Mrs Anderson from next door, and Kirsty was kept busy handing out beer and wine cup.

Everyone was chatting away and the room was quite noisy, but about twenty past eight, Penny held the door open and Gyles pushed his mother's wheelchair into the room. There was the little embarrassed silence that always falls when healthy people are suddenly faced with someone less fortunate, but Kirsty immediately put down her glass and crossed to greet them. She was aware of Gyles running his eyes over her appraisingly, but she concentrated on Mrs Grantham.

She smiled warmly and reached out to shake the older woman's hand. 'Hallo, I'm so glad that you could come.'

Her own hand was held very tightly for a moment and Kirsty pressed it reassuringly, knowing how much courage had been needed for even this short journey from the Manor. And it was clear that Mrs Grantham had made a great effort, for her hair was set in a becoming style and she had added a little make-up, as well as putting on a smart black dress. Kirsty gave her her whole attention, chatting easily about nothing in particular until the grip on her hand eased a little and the other woman was able to answer her. Mr and Mrs Reynolds came over then and Mrs Grantham was able to let go of Kirsty's hand and greet them calmly enough. Only then did Kirsty turn to Gyles. He was watching her with an expression she couldn't define and she found to her annoyance that she flushed beneath his gaze.

'Good evening, Mr Grantham. Can I get you a drink?' she asked rather stiltedly.

'Thank you. But I thought we agreed to call each other by our christian names,' he said, moving over to the drinks table with her.

'You mean you decided, don't you? I certainly don't remember agreeing to it.'

Her hand was resting on the table and suddenly he put his over it, imprisoning it. 'Kirsty,' he said softly.

To her dismay she found that her hand was trembling violently. Slowly she turned her head to look at him and saw that he was watching her with a half rueful, half exasperated look in his dark eyes. 'When are you going to stop fighting me?'

Hastily she turned away. 'We have beer and sherry, or there's wine cup, if you'd prefer it.'

He didn't answer, so that she had perforce to look at him again. He was watching her quizzically, waiting.

'Gyles,' she said unevenly.

He smiled, his eyes warm. 'Beer would be fine, thank you.'

Dave came up to greet him then, fortunately, and Kirsty was able to pour out Gyles' beer without his seeing how much she spilled because her hands were still shaking. Carefully she carried it across to him, and the smile was still in his eyes as he took it from her and immediately included her in their conversation.

'The Society's done a tremendous job on your room. A great improvement on the way it used to look.'

'Why, yes, it is, but how do you....' Then she remembered how he had torn through the house looking for his imaginary hippies, and her voice grew stiff. 'I'd forgotten that you'd seen the room before.'

'But that was a long time ago—during the war.' His eyes looked into her mockingly and she knew immediately that he was referring to their private feud. Her chin came up.

'You think it's over, then?'

'Oh, I'm sure of it. Entente is the order of the day.'

His eyes were looking deep into hers and Kirsty felt that the two of them were the only ones in the room, talking a language that no one else understood.

'How do you know it isn't just a temporary truce?'

'Because from now on I intend to make love, not war—isn't that what your contemporaries believe in?' he added after a definite pause.

Someone touched her arm and she dragged her eyes away to become aware that Penny had come up to her and that Dave was looking at them both with a mystified expression on his face. Hurriedly she said, 'Will you excuse me?' and moved aside with Penny.

'Everyone's here now except Simon,' her sister told her.

'I expect he got held up in the traffic. Come and meet Mrs Grantham properly.'

They joined the little group round Mrs Grantham's chair and chatted for a while until the elder woman caught her son's eye. Gyles went out into the hall and came back with a parcel which he handed to her.

'This is from Gyles and myself,' she told the girls. 'A house-warming present.'

They looked at her in surprise. 'Oh, but really you shouldn't have....' Kirsty began in embarrassment, but Mrs Grantham stopped her.

'It's our pleasure. Please—open it.'

Kirsty gave it to Penny and watched the younger girl excitedly taking off the ribbon and gift wrapping. Penny had always loved opening parcels and at Christmas times it had been torture for her to wait until Christmas Day. But that had been when their parents were still alive. A small ache of grief filled Kirsty for a moment and she looked away, but then Penny gave an exclamation of pleasure and Kirsty saw her taking a beautiful antique copper kettle from its box. The mellow sheen of the copper, with a polish that owed nothing to modern lacquers, caught the light and reflected it as everyone crowded round to admire it.

'We thought it might look well in your inglenook,' Mrs Grantham told them.

'Oh, it will. It's perfect,' Penny said enthusiastically, and carried it across to the huge fireplace and set it on a shelf near the front. 'There—how does that look?'

Kirsty turned to Mrs Grantham. 'Thank you, it was very thoughtful of you. We'll treasure it always.' And she impulsively leaned forward to kiss the elder woman lightly on the cheek.

'And thank *you*, my dear,' Mrs Grantham said softly.

Penny came over to add her thanks and Kirsty turned to Gyles. 'Thank you, it's a lovely present. We're very grateful to you.'

His left brow rose quizzically. 'But not as grateful as you were to my mother?'

Kirsty frowned slightly. 'We're equally grateful to you both, of course.'

'But you kissed *her*,' Gyles pointed out.

Her eyes flew to meet his, not sure whether or not he was teasing, but he was looking at her half mockingly, half expectantly, and she still didn't know, so she merely laughed politely and said, 'Let me get you another drink?'

His mouth twisted with amusement. 'Little coward! No, you circulate, I'll help myself to a drink.'

She moved away and joined a group of Society members who were discussing the possibility of opening a museum in Barham, but after a while she looked at her watch rather worriedly; already nine o'clock and Simon still hadn't arrived. Soon Penny came up to her and wanted to know when they were going to serve the food.

'Give him ten more minutes and then we'll just have to serve it.'

She was becoming increasingly worried, her imagination working overtime with mental pictures of terrible accidents and the possible consequences. She was standing talking to Dave when Gyles strolled over and joined them. He asked her how the herb farm was progressing, but Kirsty answered him rather abstractedly. She glanced at her watch again; nearly half past nine, and she bit her lip anxiously. Eyes narrowed, Gyles went to speak to her, but just then the knocker sounded and looking across at Penny as she hurried to answer it, Kirsty gave a sigh of relief.

When he came into the room, Simon paused a moment on the threshold, looking round for her. He looked very handsome in a well-cut navy velvet jacket, and he appeared quite unruffled by any embarrassment at his late arrival. Kirsty waited for her heart to swell at the sight of him, to feel excitement running through her veins, but apart from the feeling of relief that he had arrived safely, there was nothing—absolutely nothing!

Catching sight of her, he walked across and put his hands on her shoulders. 'Hallo, darling.' Then he bent and kissed her on the mouth.

Kirsty expected the usual thrill at his touch, but again she felt nothing and stepped quickly away. 'You're late. I was worried you'd had an accident.'

'No, nothing like that. There was a bit of a get-together after the match and I couldn't get away.'

'Couldn't you have telephoned? You must have known that Kirsty would be worried about you.'

To her surprise Gyles had intervened and there was a rather harsh look in his eyes. Hastily she introduced them. 'Our neighbour, Gyles Grantham. And this is Dr Simon Granger, a friend.'

Simon laughed. 'She means her boy-friend, but she's too shy to say it. And Kirsty needn't have worried—she knew I'd turn up some time tonight.' He put his arm round her waist and possessively pulled her to him to kiss her again. Immediately Gyles turned away, his mouth set into a thin line.

Flushing hotly, Kirsty pulled away from Simon and went to get him a drink, although she strongly suspected that he'd had one or two already. Immediately after that they served the food and she was kept busy for quite a time before she had a chance to get Simon on his own and whisper, 'Talk to Mrs Grantham for me—she's in the wheelchair. See if she'll tell you anything about her condition.'

He looked at her indignantly. '*That* wasn't what you got me down here for, was it?'

'No. No, that was something else entirely. Please, Simon.'

He shrugged rather irritably. 'Oh, all right.'

Kirsty watched him go and give Mrs Grantham his charming smile and hook forward a chair to sit beside her, setting himself to win her over. And he probably would, too. Standing a little apart from everyone, she glanced from Simon to Gyles, who was talking to Mr Reynolds on the other side of the room. His face in profile seemed hard and autocratic until she remembered the warmth in his eyes when he had smiled at her earlier that evening. Slowly she looked from one to the other of the two men again, both unaware of her scrutiny. It seemed a very strange time and place to discover that she had got over an infatuation for one man, only to fall headlong in love with another!

At about eleven the party began to break up, Gyles and his mother being among the first to leave.

'Goodnight, my dear, and thank you for a very pleasant evening. I've enjoyed myself immensely,' Mrs Grantham said with a smile.

'You must come whenever you feel like it,' Kirsty replied warmly. She straightened and looked at Gyles rather shyly.

He nodded brusquely, 'Thank you. Goodnight,' and turned abruptly away to push his mother through the doorway.

Feeling rather numb, Kirsty stared after him, completely bewildered by his attitude, but just then someone else came up to say goodnight and she was kept busy until everyone, except Simon, had gone.

There was the usual rather flat feeling one experiences when faced with the aftermath of a party. Penny looked tired, so Kirsty made her go to bed while she cleared up the debris and washed the dishes and glasses.

Simon lounged in a chair and chatted to her about the latest hospital gossip until she'd finished, then he rose languidly and yawned. 'Think I'll go on up. Which room have you put me in?'

'I'll show you.' She dried her hands and preceded him up the stairs, taking him into the bedroom that she had been using and switching on the light. 'We haven't got round to decorating this room, I'm afraid. Have you got everything you need?'

She moved towards the window to close the curtains, but Simon caught hold of her before she reached it. He put his hands low on her waist and pulled her to him. 'Everything except you,' he said thickly, and sought her lips to kiss her ardently.

Kirsty let him do so because she still couldn't quite believe that there was nothing there any more; she had thought herself in love with him for months. But his kiss had lost all its power to turn her on and somehow it seemed wrong to even let him touch her. Abruptly she drew away and put her hands against his chest, holding him off.

'Hey!' His voice was indignant and he tried to pull her close again.

'Did—did Mrs Grantham talk to you?' she asked, hoping to distract him.

'What? Oh, yes, she told me a little, but it would be impossible to tell whether an operation or the new electrical treatment for bone setting would be of any use to her until she'd been examined by an expert and had up-to-date X-rays.'

'But you think there could be a chance for her?' Kirsty persisted.

Simon shrugged. 'As I said, I'm no expert, but any-thing's worth a try.'

'I remember there's quite a lot of literature on the new methods in the hospital library. Will you send me copies so that I can show them to her?'

'Sure. *Now* can we get back to us?' His arms tight-ened and he kissed her again, then withdrew one arm to seek the fastening of her dress. 'Darling, I want you so much. Stay with me tonight.'

Immediately Kirsty pushed him away. 'No. No, I can't.' She turned her back to him and stood at the window while she tried to collect her thoughts. She must tell him now, once and for all, it would be cruel to let him go on thinking that she cared for him. And foolish too—because tonight Simon seemed set on tak-ing things further than they had ever gone before.

He came up behind her and put his arms round her, murmuring something into her neck. Kirsty squared her shoulders to tell him, but as she went to turn round she noticed a pinpoint of light in the lane below the house and realised that someone was stand-ing there, smoking a cigarette. As she watched the moon came out for a minute and she was able to see more clearly. It was Gyles. He was standing looking up at the window, and she knew with the utmost cer-tainty that he must have seen everything, silhouetted as they were with the light behind them. And the con-clusions he would reach were sickeningly obvious. As Kirsty stared down at him, transfixed with shock, he threw down his cigarette and turned abruptly away to stride back up the lane.

CHAPTER SEVEN

THE next day was a hard one to get through. Kirsty had told Simon as gently as she knew how, that she was very sorry but her feelings had changed towards him. At first he had been incredulous and then blazingly angry. He tried to use sex as a weapon and to kiss and caress her into saying she hadn't meant it, but she had stubbornly refused to respond and had pushed him away.

He stared at her, his eyes furious. 'What the hell did you get me down here for, then? You said you needed me.'

'I needed to *see* you,' Kirsty told him in some distress. 'I wasn't sure in my own mind whether or not I still felt anything—anything serious for you. And as soon as I saw you I—I knew that I didn't. I'm sorry.'

Simon looked at her grimly. 'There's someone else, isn't there?'

She nodded, unable to speak.

He turned away, 'It's my own fault. I should never have let you come down here, I should have insisted you stay in London.'

'You could hardly have stopped me,' she pointed out rather defiantly.

'Oh, yes, I could. Because you were in love with me then. I should have taken you to bed when I had the chance, so that you'd have been committed to me,' he said harshly.

Kirsty flushed but said firmly, 'I thought I was in love with you, but it wasn't the real thing—an infatuation, if you like. And only a pale comparison to what I feel now.'

His mouth twisted. 'Who's the lucky man?'

'Does it matter?'

His jaw tightened. 'No, I don't suppose it does. You'd better get out of here before I get angry again and forget myself. I'll leave first thing in the morning.'

Kirsty looked at him miserably, deeply aware of his hurt. 'Simon, I'm sorry, I....'

'For God's sake stop saying that and get out of here!'

Hastily she went, to pass a night as sleepless as Simon's. She knew she had done the right thing, but could imagine how she would have felt if their positions had been reversed. Added to which was her worry about Gyles' possible reaction to what he had seen. He was bound to put the very worst interpretation on it—and just as they seemed to be establishing some sort of contact, too. It couldn't have happened at a worse time.

Simon was as good as his word and left immediately after breakfast. He seemed resigned, but Kirsty noticed that he deliberately avoided touching her or getting too close to her, and the look he gave her when he left spoke volumes, so that she felt guilty and miserable for hours afterwards. Dave called round to take Penny out and Kirsty walked up to the little wood on top of the hill, half hoping that Gyles might see her and join her, but although she stayed there for quite a long time he didn't appear and she walked disconsolately home again.

That night she again lay awake, wondering how she could possibly let Gyles know that he had been mistaken, that there had never been anything more than a few kisses between her and Simon. But how could you go up to a man and tell him a thing like that? And anyway he was probably so disgusted that he would take care never to see her again. Kirsty turned restlessly on the pillow. Should she go and call on his mother in the hope of seeing him? Or would that be too obvious? She felt suddenly very young and defenceless and wished she had someone to turn to for advice. She was so afraid of making a fool of herself; with Simon she had known how to behave, their relationship had been easy and natural and she hadn't been afraid to show that she liked him, but now.... Whenever she thought of Gyles she was filled with a sense of exhilarating excitement, but mixed with it was fear, fear that he was only being neighbourly and condescending. He had said himself how young she was and this made her afraid of what his reaction might be if she ever dared to show him that she cared.

And she did care—so much. She supposed it must have been there all along, all the time she was quarrelling with him, but she had only realised just what it was when she had seen Gyles and Simon together. And now all the confidence she had been beginning to gain as a woman was gone, she was unsure of herself and so vulnerable that even a harsh look from Gyles could keep her awake all night like this.

But she fell into a troubled sleep at last and dreamt that the cows that had died had come back to haunt her, their pitiful ululation seeming to be all around her bed.

'Kirsty! Kirsty, wake up!' She came to her senses with a start to realise that Penny, still in her nightclothes, was shaking her vigorously.

'What? What is it, what's wrong?' Kirsty stared at her stupidly, still half asleep.

'Look out of the window. Oh, come on, quickly!' Penny said impatiently while she groped for her mules.

Obediently Kirsty stumbled to the window as Penny pushed it open. It was still very early, the sun hadn't yet completely climbed over the horizon. She looked out and was instantly fully awake. 'Oh no!'

There were about a dozen cows in the garden placidly eating away at their young plants and trampling the others into the ground. Behind them the gate into the field stood wide open.

'Oh no!' Kirsty groaned again, then ran to scramble into her clothes. 'Come on, we'll have to chase them out.'

They armed themselves with long sticks and waved their arms at the creatures, shouting at them and trying to drive them towards the gate, but as soon as they got one out and went for another, the first one would come back.

'You'll just have to stand by the gate, Penny, and open it whenever I manage to drive one towards you,' Kirsty yelled. But the wretched animals would determinedly go off in the opposite direction whenever she thought she had one cornered, and it took over an hour before they got them all out, by which time Kirsty was heartily cursing them.

Together they stood and surveyed the shambles that had once been their neat garden. The plants were almost totally eaten, the young seedlings completely ruined, and even the brick paths that Kirsty had so carefully laid had been broken or pushed out of place by the heavy feet of the cattle. Kirsty looked down at the bottom of the gate, and it came as no surprise to see that the earth and plants that had built up round the bottom because it hadn't been used for years, had been dug away so that it could be opened.

Penny followed her gaze and burst into tears, then whirled on the elder girl. 'I thought you said he wanted to be friendly? We even asked him to our party and still he does this to us! The two-faced hypocrite!'

Kirsty stared at her aghast. 'But surely you don't think that Gyles did this?'

'Of course he did. Who else wants us out? You told me yourself that he sent someone along to try to buy this place for him. If you ask me, he was just using the commune idea as an excuse, and now that's out he's willing to resort to any underhand trick to get rid of us,' she added vehemently.

'That's ridiculous,' Kirsty retorted. 'You've forgotten that the farmer and his men were just as angry with us. Anyone could have come and opened the gate, even one of the young boys in the village could have done it as a prank. You can't go around accusing Gyles without evidence. I won't have it,' she insisted.

Penny regarded her angrily. 'You're very quick to stand up for him. You haven't got a crush on him, have you?'

Kirsty flushed and hastily disclaimed, 'No, of course not. I just don't believe that he'd do this to us, that's all. What possible reason could he have to....' She stopped abruptly, remembering how he'd seen her with Simon. But no, he might be angry but surely he wouldn't stoop to something as petty as this?

Penny seized on her hesitation. 'You see? You've got to admit that everything points to Gyles Grantham.' She added furiously, 'I've a good mind to go and tell him what I think of him.'

'Well, you won't,' Kirsty said forcibly. 'Do you understand me, Penny? You'll say nothing about this to anyone, not even Dave. And I don't want to hear another word against the Squire or anyone else, because that would only create further trouble. We're just going to nail up that gate so that it can't possibly happen again and then we'll straighten up the garden and buy new plants and seeds. And then we're going to forget about the whole thing, put it completely out of our minds. Now come and help me get started,' she commanded.

For a moment the younger girl stard at her defiantly, her mouth mulish, but then she shrugged. 'Oh, all right, if that's the way you want it. But it doesn't mean that I've changed my mind. I still believe the Squire is responsible for everything that's happened to us.'

They worked hard on the garden all morning, saving what plants they could and relaying the paths, and in the early afternoon Kirsty phoned the herb suppliers and arranged to collect more plants. They set off at once, but had only got about ten miles along the road when the engine of the van started to make weird noises. Pulling into the side, Kirsty checked to see that the fan belt was still in place and could find nothing wrong. She looked at the engine rather helplessly, wishing she knew more about what made the thing go.

'Perhaps it needs some oil?' Penny suggested.

'It looks all right,' Kirsty told her, examining the dip-stick. 'But I think we'd better pull into the next garage and let a mechanic look at it.'

The road they were on, however, was long and empty and after only a couple of miles the engine gave out completely and they coasted into the curb.

'Oh, no, this is all we need!' Kirsty looked around but could see no houses in sight. 'You'd better stay with the van while I walk to the nearest phone. Cheer up,' she added, seeing Penny's woebegone face. 'It's probably something quite simple.'

But when she finally reached a house with a phone and contacted a garage with a repair service the mechanic shook his head. 'Sorry, miss, but she's seized up solid. You won't get another mile out of her.'

'But what caused it?' Kirsty asked in dismay.

He grimaced non-committally. 'Can't say until you take the engine down and examine it. What are you going to do?'

'Why don't we phone Dave?' Penny suggested. 'He's got a breakdown truck.'

So the mechanic gave them a lift to the nearest phone box where they waited for Dave to come and collect them and take the van in tow back to his garage, promising to look at it straight away. But they were both tired and dispirited by the time they got home.

The next morning they went round to the garage, hopefully expecting Dave to have worked miracles so that they could go and pick up the plants, but they knew at once from his serious face that they weren't going to get that lucky.

'Sorry, but I'm afraid it's quite a big job. The engine will have to be taken out, stripped down and cleaned.'

'But what on earth's wrong with it?' Kirsty demanded. 'A new engine was put in just before I bought it.'

Dave looked uncomfortable. 'I'm afraid someone put sugar in the gas tank. It's fatal once it gets through to the engine. It seizes up all the moving parts completely.'

They stared at him appalled, then Penny turned to Kirsty, her face pinched with fury. 'Now see what's happened! I told you he'd do anything to get rid of us, but you wouldn't listen to me. We've got to....'

But Kirsty stopped her before she could finish. 'Penny, be quiet! We'll talk about this later.'

Looking from one to the other of them, Dave said, 'Look, if you girls have any idea who did this you should go to the police.'

'No, we haven't,' Kirsty said hastily. 'Penny was just jumping to conclusions.' She tried to speak more calmly. 'Can you fix the engine for us? How long do you think it will take?'

'At least two weeks. The parts will all have to be soaked in an acid solution and cleaned individually before they can be put back again.'

'As long as that? But we have to go and collect some plants.'

'Well, I can lend you my van this afternoon, if you like, but I can't let you have it indefinitely because I shall need it myself.'

'Oh, that's marvellous. Thanks a lot, Dave,' Kirsty said warmly. She hesitated. 'How much will the engine cost?'

Dave shrugged. 'Well over a hundred pounds, I'm afraid, and that's cutting it to a minimum.'

'That does it, then,' Kirsty said tiredly. 'We can't possibly afford such a big bill. We'll just have to sell the van as it stands and manage without one. Can we leave it here until we find a buyer?'

'Sure, but you'll be lucky if you find anyone to take it as it is.' He looked at them frowningly. 'Look, I've got an idea. Come into the office, both of you.'

He led them into a cubbyhole at the back of the garage with a desk that was piled high with files and bits of paper, a lot of which had spread on to the floor and windowsill. Dave shut the door and turned to them. 'Can either of you do office work? Filing and simple book-keeping, that kind of thing?'

The girls glanced at one another. 'I suppose we both can,' Penny answered.

'Good. Then how about making a bargain? I'll repair your van if one of you will come here for two or three days a week and sort this lot out. I used to have a retired bank clerk to do it, but he became ill. Now I try to keep it down myself, but I just don't have the time. And when you've worked off the cost of the repairs we can review the situation. Well, what do you think?'

'We think it's a terrific idea, don't we, Penny?' Kirsty said promptly. 'And Penny must be the one to take it on because she's more experienced with office work than I am, and not only that, she's still not really well enough to work in the garden, but this will be ideal for her. Thanks, Dave, we're really very grateful,' she added sincerely.

But Dave was looking at Penny, who had a bright flush to her cheeks at the thought of spending far more time in his company. Kirsty grinned; she knew darn well that she could have done the job just as easily, but the idea wouldn't have been anywhere near as popular, and she wondered what the outcome of the arrangement would be.

They started to discuss the details of the scheme, but Kirsty left them to it and wandered into the workshop to stand and gaze gloomily at their van, which looked somehow forlorn with its hood up and various bits of its engine removed. Letting the cows into their garden she could think of as a childish prank, even though it would cost them a lot of money and set back all the work they had done almost to the beginning, but to put sugar in their gas tank was nothing short of criminal. And she couldn't believe that a child would have the sort of knowledge to do such a thing. Also they parked the van at the front of the house all the time, so it was more than likely that it had been done under cover of darkness, which again ruled out young children. Which left only one conclusion and

one that she had been vainly trying not to reach; that
Penny was right and that someone was using every
dirty trick they could think of to try and get rid of
them. The very thought that anyone could hate them
so much made her cringe inside. Miserably she wandered out to the front of the garage and sat on a low
wall while she looked round her at the old church and
the village green with its silver birch trees full of
bright green new leaves. They could have been so
happy here. Why, oh, why was it happening to them?

Slowly she got up and walked across the green, past
the drinking fountain that didn't work any more, past
the patch of bare earth between two young trees that
had been planted inadvertently, but very conveniently, at just the right distance apart for the village
boys to use them as goalposts. The door of the church
stood ajar and she pushed it open and went in. Inside it was simple but beautiful. Its main adornment
was a stained-glass window over the altar, the rich
colours of the glass still glowing strong and bright after
five hundred years. There were memorial tablets set
into the walls, many of them bearing the names of
long-dead Granthams, and set into the floor of the
nave she found an engraved brass with the figures of a
knight and his lady dated 1347 and, although the let-
tering was worn, when she knelt and ran her fingers
over it she could make out the name Gyles Grantham.
So there had been Granthams at Notley even then?
Lifting her head, she looked up at the altar and silently
begged: Don't let it be him. Please, please, don't let
it be him, with such an intensity of feeling that she
almost spoke aloud.

But although she might wish for Gyles' innocence
with all her heart, the facts all seemed to point directly
to him. Over the next few days she thought of little

else, but always she came back to the same question: who else could it be? Diligently she put in the new plants, but by now she was in a state of nerves and was constantly on the alert for some other trick to be played on them, and wondering dispiritedly if she was doing the right thing in staying on. The herb garden was as much Penny's as her own and it was hardly fair on the younger girl if she insisted on staying at the cottage and spending more money on it, only to have something else go wrong so that they would have to admit themselves beaten and leave in the end anyway. But surely whoever it was—she still couldn't bring herself to accuse Gyles—would realise that they weren't going to be pushed out and leave them alone now.

As the days passed uneventfully, Kirsty became a little more optimistic. Penny had started her job at the garage, working Monday, Wednesday and Friday, and seemed to be enjoying it, coming home smiling and often going out with Dave in the evenings to the cinema or a disco in Barham. Kirsty herself travelled there one day to visit the bank and do some shopping. Towards the end of the afternoon she was standing in the market square waiting for the bus back to Notley when to her consternation Gyles pulled up in his Range-Rover.

'Jump in, I'm going back to the village.' He leant across to push the passenger door open for her.

As coolly as she could, Kirsty answered, 'Thanks, but the bus will be along in a minute,' and she shut the door again and turned her back to stare with a sudden interest into a nearby shop window.

For a moment there was silence, but instead of the engine starting up, she heard the other door open and brisk footsteps coming towards her. Her pulse started to race and she could feel the hairs at the back of her neck start to prickle with fright. Gyles caught hold of her arm and spun her round to face him, his face taut with anger.

'Get in the car!'

'No, I'd rather go on the bus.' Defiantly she glared at him.

His jaw thrust forward menacingly. 'Are you going to get in the car or do I have to *put* you in?'

Briefly she continued to defy him, but the grip on her arm tightened and he stepped forward, his eyes dangerous. Reluctantly she capitulated and bent to pick up her basket.

'Very well, since you give me no choice.' Head high, she got into the car, only then becoming aware that they were being watched with avid curiosity by everyone else in the line-up.

Gyles got in beside her but didn't glance her way as he pulled away and drove out of the town. Kirsty sat stiffly in her seat, her gaze fixed out of the window, but she was acutely aware of him and had to grip her hands tightly together in her lap to stop them from shaking. After a while it penetrated to her brain that he had taken a different turning from the main road and she didn't recognise her surroundings at all. She opened her mouth to say, Where are you taking me? but it sounded so corny that she shut it again and the strained silence continued between them. At first Kirsty thought he must be taking a short cut she didn't know about, but gradually she became increasingly uneasy, especially when he turned off the road into a lane that was little better than a track and seemed to lead only into a field, where he pulled up.

The silence seemed very loud then and Kirsty stared fixedly out of the windscreen, too proud to ask him where they were. She knew that he was studying her, but still she wouldn't look round. Then he said with scarcely controlled anger, 'And now perhaps you wouldn't mind telling me what the hell that was all about back there?'

Keeping her voice cold, she replied, 'I told you, I wanted to go on the bus.'

'You didn't want to come with me, you mean.'

Kirsty didn't answer and he muttered something under his breath. Then she heard him get out and he came and held her door open for her.

'Let's take a walk. There are the ruins of an old castle just over here.'

Slowly she swung her legs out and stood up. For a moment their eyes met, but she looked quickly away, her heart thudding. There was a path across the field and they went along it, Kirsty taking care to walk a little in front so that her arm didn't accidentally touch him. They came to a stile which she climbed nimbly over and then she saw the age-old stones of the remains of what must have been a large castle, probably Norman from the shape of the windows and the one doorway that was left standing. For a little while they walked round it, still not speaking, but then they came to a part looking out over the valley below and Gyles stopped.

Kirsty turned to him impatiently. 'Can we go back now?'

'Not yet. I want to know why you didn't want to come with me today.'

Anger rose in her at that because she was still unsure of him, and afraid to let him see how she felt, so she took refuge in attack and said caustically, 'I should have thought that was obvious. I don't like peeping Toms.'

'What the hell do you mean by that?'

'You know darn well what I mean! I *saw* you on the night of our party when you were looking up at my window.'

Gyles stepped closer, his face a mask of anger. 'And you, with your suspicious little mind, immediately jumped to the nastiest conclusion you could think of. Well, just to put the record straight, I often take an evening stroll down the lane. It's hardly my fault if you happened to see me passing when your doctor friend was practising his bedside manner on you!' he bit out viciously.

'Why, you....' Driven by uncontrollable indignation, Kirsty lifted her hand to hit him, but he moved too fast for her and caught her wrist. For a brief second his eyes blazed at her and then he pulled her roughly against him, his mouth fastening on hers compulsively as he kissed her with a fierce, burning intensity. At first she was so startled that she let him do what he wanted, but even as she began to stiffen he lifted his head and looked at her, a strange expression in his dark eyes.

'I've been wanting to do that for a hell of a long time,' he said, his voice uneven.

Kirsty looked away, afraid of her own emotions, and tried to speak offhandedly. 'And now you've done it. So what?'

'So now I'm going to do it again.'

And he did, more gently to begin with as he explored her mouth, his lips hard against her own, but then becoming more importuning, more demanding, forcing her lips apart. Kirsty was aware of his strength, of his arms crushing her to him, moulding her body against his. She tried to resist him, to stand cold and rigid under the hot demands of his mouth, but the mental and physical temptation to give in to him was

the strongest feeling she had ever known. Her body
trembled, touched against his lean hardness, and suddenly she gave a little moan and began to respond,
her arms going round his neck, her body moving sen-
suously against him. Her submission could only in-
flame his senses even further and he kissed her so
passionately that he hurt her, his lips only leaving her
bruised mouth when he began to explore her throat,
the curve of her neck, her eyes.

When at last he let her go her legs were so unsteady
that she had to lean back against the wall, the stones
cool against her burning skin. Gyles still had hold of
her arms but his touch was gentle now, his hands caressing.

'Kirsty, look at me,' he commanded, his voice still
thick and ragged.

Slowly she raised her head and saw such a light of
triumph in his dark eyes that she was afraid. She feared
that responding to him so ardently might make him
realise how much she loved him and she didn't know
how to handle the situation. She waited with beating
heart for him to say something, to give some indication
that he felt anything more than just desire for her, but
he merely bent to kiss her again and she immediately
turned her head away.

'*Now* can we get back to Notley?' she asked, keeping her voice as cold as she cold.

She felt him stiffen and draw away a little. 'Now?'

'Of course. Why not now?'

'Because a minute ago you were in my arms, that's
why not!' He put his hand under her chin and forced
her to face him.

Kirsty willed herself to look at him calmly. She must
try to keep him at arm's length, she knew that if he
kissed her again she was lost. With a disdainful little

laugh she said, 'You don't really think that a few kisses mean anything to someone of my generation, do you?'

His eyes burned into hers and she could feel her heart do crazy flip-flops in her chest. Oh, God, if only she could be sure of him! Slowly he straightened up, his face set in an unreadable mask. 'Evidently not.' His voice colder than winter ice, he reached in his pocket for his cigarette case. 'So why let me kiss you at all?'

'I could hardly stop you,' Kirsty replied rather tartly.

'But you didn't have to—co-operate the way you did.'

She managed to shrug airily. 'I just wondered what it would be like to be kissed by an older man, that's all.'

There was a sudden shattering silence and Kirsty stood with beating heart, staring out over the valley, her emotions in shreds.

When Gyles spoke his voice was almost a snarl. 'And did I come up to your expectations?'

It took an immense effort, but she forced herself to turn and face him, a small amused smile on her lips. 'Do you really want me to answer that?'

His face grew bleak. 'No, I don't suppose I do.' He turned abruptly away, drawing viciously on the cigarette.

The silence lengthened and became unbearable. Kirsty sought desperately for something to break it. 'Those are most unusual cigarettes,' she managed at last. 'I've never seen any black ones before.'

For a moment he didn't answer, then he said shortly, 'They're Turkish. I discovered them when I was abroad one year and I have them sent to me from Paris.' He turned and began to walk back towards the car, Kirsty following, but at the stile he stopped again and turned towards her.

Curtly he said, 'The reason I brought you here was because I wanted an opportunity to thank you for the help and encouragement you've given my mother. She was fast becoming a recluse and nothing I tried to do made any difference, but whatever you said to her seemed to have the right effect, because she's been out several times since. I'm extremely grateful,' he added stiffly.

But Kirsty was looking at him in some surprise. 'You realised what was the matter with her?'

He frowned. 'I'm not completely insensitive to other people, especially my own mother,' he answered bitingly.

Kirsty flushed. 'I'm sure you're not. It's just that she thought she kept everything hidden from you so well.' She paused and then said hesitatingly, 'Your mother told me something of her accident; it's been quite a long time since she had a thorough check-up, and medical science has progressed enormously in that field recently. Don't you think it would be a good idea if she tried the new treatments?'

Gyles looked at her sharply. 'Have you suggested this to her?' And when Kirsty shook her head, he went on forcefully, 'Then don't. She's had too many disappointments in the past and I don't want her hurt again, especially now when she's starting to come to terms with her handicap.'

'But if there's a chance, then....'

'No, Kirsty. Under no circumstances will I let her subject herself to more painful operations and treatments. You don't know what she's suffered in the past. My father tried everything to get her cured, she spent years in hospitals, but it only left her worse than she was in the beginning. And I don't want her lifted by false hopes only to have them dashed again. 'You're to promise me that you'll say nothing to her, do you understand?' he demanded.

'But you know nothing about the new electrical treatments.'

'And you do, I suppose?' he said caustically.

'Yes, as it happens, I do. Before we came to Notley I was the librarian at a London teaching hospital, and it was my job to keep up to date with every kind of medical breakthrough. And not only that, Simon talked to your mother and he said that....'

'Simon? You had the temerity to discuss my mother with your boy-friend?' he demanded harshly.

'Well, he *is* a doctor—and a darn good one,' Kirsty retorted, becoming angry.

Gyles glared at her. 'I forbid you to even mention this to my mother. Do you hear me, Kirsty? You're to promise here and now never to speak to her about it.'

Kirsty's face was very pale, but she faced him steadily. 'Oh, I hear you all right. But I'd like to know just what right you have to make a decision like that when your mother is capable of making up her own mind?'

His face darkened and he took a swift step towards her, but fortunately a minibus drew into the field just then and a crowd of noisy schoolchildren began to clamber out. Hastily Kirsty climbed over the stile and walked to where the car was parked. She was afraid that he would try to force her to promise, but he evidently decided that she would obey him and didn't pursue the matter, turning on the radio as soon as he got into the car.

Coldly he told her, 'I have to go to the garden centre on the way back, but it won't take more than a few minutes.'

When they got there he invited her to come inside, but she refused and stayed in the car, nodding briefly to the manager's surprised greeting when he came out with Gyles and saw her waiting for him.

The taut silence between them during the rest of the drive back to the cottage was broken only when Gyles said, 'Is your sister using your van today?'

Stiffly Kirsty answered, 'No, it's broken down.'

'Anything serious?'

'Something wrong with the engine.' And how, she thought bitterly. Then wondered miserably for the thousandth time if the man sitting beside her, who had held her in his arms and kissed her so passionately, was indeed responsible for all their troubles. If only she knew beyond doubt that he was innocent! Then she would have been able to respond without the fear that she was making a fool of herself, without the dreadful thought at the back of her mind that he was sadistically trying to make her fall for him only because it gave added spice to the vendetta he was waging against them.

When they got to the cottage she got out without waiting for him to open the door for her, said shortly, 'Thanks for the lift,' and walked down the path without a backward glance.

Two days later a bulky envelope arrived containing photostats of all the information she had wanted from the hospital library, together with a short note from Simon. There was no personal word to Kirsty herself, no mention of anything that had been between them, for which she was profoundly thankful. She read over the photostats carefully and then read Simon's note again. 'I must stress that a thorough examination would have to be carried out before it could be decided which, if any, of these treatments might be of benefit to Mrs Grantham.' And he went on to list several consultants who were the top men in that particular field and whom Mrs Grantham might consult.

Kirsty sat for a long time, torn between a wish to show them to Mrs Grantham because she sincerely believed that it was the older woman's right to choose and no one else's, that only she could decide whether the pain and possible failure were worth the risk if there was the remotest chance of success, and the knowledge that by doing so she would alienate Gyles even further. If he were innocent of everything else this wouldn't matter so much to anyone except her, it would only make him even more angry with her than he was already, but if he were guilty, if he really was responsible for all the dirty tricks that had been played on them.... Kirsty's mind shrank from the thought of what form his anger might take. Dare she take the risk? Could anything possibly justify her deliberately taking the chance of putting their livelihood in jeopardy again?

But there was no choice really, she had known what her decision would be all along. Taking out her pen, she wrote a covering letter and put it in the envelope with the photostats and Simon's note, then she waited until she saw Gyles go out before she took it up to the Manor and asked the butler to give it to Mrs Grantham personally. Once it was done, she felt a great surge of relief. Now the responsibility was no longer hers and it was up to Mrs Grantham to decide what she wanted to do. Perhaps the handicapped woman might be as angry with her as Gyles had been, but that, too, Kirsty could bear if she had to.

She continued to work methodically on the garden, Penny helping her when she wasn't at the garage, and now the place was really beginning to look cared for.

At last they had managed to cut back all the rest of the hedges and had heaped all the cuttings into a pile ready to burn. The front garden, too, was starting to look better as the wallflowers came out and the buds began to appear on the climbing rose round the doorway. Kirsty looked at them every day, eager to see what colour they would be. Penny was sure they would be red, but she thought white.

Late one afternoon, a week or so after she'd sent the photostats to Mrs Grantham, Kirsty decided to light the bonfire. She was almost an old hand at this now and stood and watched as the twigs crackled and burned. There was very little wind, the smoke rising almost straight into the sky. It had been an unusually warm day for May and she wore just a sun-top and denim shorts, her skin already beginning to tan from spending so many hours out of doors. Penny was still at the garage and Kirsty stood alone, leaning on a spade, ready to beat out any spark that leapt from the crackling flames, not that there was much chance of that on such a still day.

The sound of a car door slamming and brisk footsteps coming up the garden path made her look up, and then the blood drained from her face as she saw Gyles walk round the side of the house, one look at his face revealing that he was furiously angry. Defensively she gripped the spade and held it in front of her. He came quickly across the grass and stopped just a few feet away. His eyes were as cold as water over stone. Involuntarily she stepped away from him, and his lips curled in a snarl of anger.

Harshly he bit out, 'Yes, you're right to move away from me, because if I once lay my hands on you I won't answer for the consequences!' He glared across at her, fists clenched, only an iron will-power stopping him from catching hold of her and shaking her viciously. 'Do you know what your meddling has done?' he demanded savagely. 'My mother went to see a specialist without telling me, and now she's determined to go ahead with a course of treatment if it's at all possible. To go through all that pain, suffering, hope, and then despair again! And just because an interfering little fool put the idea into her head. And after you'd promised me that you wouldn't say anything to her!'

'Stop it!' Kirsty shouted at him. 'I didn't make any promises. You just ordered me not to and took it for granted that I'd obey you. But I bet you've never stopped to look at it from your mother's point of view. Do you know what it's like to be imprisoned in a wheelchair, to be entirely dependent on other people for your every need? All there is is hope. Hope that the next cure will be the right one, or the one after that. Your mother had given up hoping, that was why she was letting herself just fade away. And you were to blame, because you were the one who'd taken hope away from her, condemned her to stay in that wheelchair for the rest of her life because you were too much of a coward to let her keep on trying. It was you who couldn't bear the pain and suffering, not her!'

His eyes murderous, Gyles took two steps towards her, unable to control himself any longer. Wrenching the spade from her he flung it contemptuously out of the way. Kirsty put up her hands in a futile attempt to defend herself, but he caught her wrists, twisting them cruelly so that she gave a cry of pain. His mouth curled in satisfaction.

'I could kill you for what you've done. You officious, do-gooding little bitch! If you were a man I'd beat the hell out of you. Everything was planned for this cottage, but you had to come along and buy it when I wasn't here to stop you.' His mouth twisted viciously. 'I tried to get rid of you by every means I knew, but you wouldn't go, would you? And now you've deliberately defied me.' His eyes burned into hers and his grip on her wrists tightened as he slowly forced her down on to her knees, taking a sadistic kind of pleasure in his power over her.

Kirsty exerted all her strength to try to resist him, but she might as well have tried to break free from an iron vice. She knelt on the ground, gazing up into his furious face, too frightened even to scream, and more terrified than she had ever been in her life. She became very still, hardly daring to breathe.

For a long moment he stared down at her, then he suddenly straightened, letting go of her wrists abruptly. His face twisted as if with pain. 'God, why the hell did you have to come here?' he groaned almost in a tone of desperation.

And then he turned and strode away, leaving her kneeling on the grass and gazing after him, the wood smoke still drifting lazily into the air.

CHAPTER EIGHT

WHEN Penny came home she found Kirsty sitting at the kitchen table, just staring blankly down at the surface, her face pale and wan.

'Why, Kirsty, what is it? Don't you feel well?'

'What?' Kirsty lifted her head abstractedly. 'Oh. No, it's just a headache, that's all.'

She tried to pull herself together and help to prepare a meal, but when they sat down to eat she made only a desultory attempt to pick at the food before pushing the plate away.

'I'm sorry, Penny, I don't feel very hungry.' She put her elbows on the table and leant her head on her hands.

Her sister looked at her in concern. 'Perhaps you've caught a bug or something. Why don't you take a couple of aspirins and have an early night?'

'Yes, I—I think I will, if you don't mind.'

She went upstairs and Penny brought her a glass of water and the tablets.

'Kirsty, is something troubling you? It isn't Simon, is it? I know you only came here to help me and that Simon wanted you to go back to London. You didn't break up because of me, did you? Because you wouldn't leave me?' The younger girl frowned unhappily. 'I couldn't bear to think that you'd lost Simon for that reason, and I'm not going to let you do it. We'll put the cottage on the market straight away and with any luck we'll get our money back on it so that we can get another flat in London. I'll go to an estate agent first thing in the morning,' she added determinedly.

Kirsty put down the glass and caught her hand. 'Hey, hold your horses! Simon and I broke up for the simple reason that I realised I didn't care for him any more. Even if we went back to London I wouldn't want to date him again. It's over completely.' She managed a wan smile. 'So don't let's have any more talk about leaving Notley. And anyway, I've an idea that Dave just might have something to say about that.'

Penny blushed and laughingly agreed, then, reassured, drew the curtains and left her alone.

The aspirins didn't seem to do any good at all; the pain in Kirsty's head gradually grew worse as she lay awake, her mind full of regrets and unhappiness. If only she could have met Gyles under different circumstances, if only they hadn't quarrelled from the beginning. But 'if only' was the most useless phrase in the English language. She'd just got to face the fact that the whole thing was hopeless and had been from the start. Even if they had met under more favourable circumstances, Gyles wouldn't have been interested in her. He was rich and well-born. What would he want with an ordinary girl more than ten years his junior? He would probably end up by marrying some rich girl from his own circle who would know how to run his home and behave correctly as the Squire's wife, Kirsty thought dismally.

But even though he would never be interested in her as a wife, the way he had kissed her at the ruined castle had certainly shown that he was fully aware of her sexually. The memory of those kisses came back to torment her now, sending a fierce surge of sexuality through her and making her body ache with longing, so that she turned and dug her fingers hard into the pillow to try to still her emotions. Surely he must have felt something for her to have kissed her like that? But then she remembered that he had done so only after he had seen Simon in her bedroom. He must have thought then that she was cheap, and decided to take advantage of her himself. And instead of resisting him as she should have done she had only added to his bad impression of her by responding to his kisses. Miserably she tossed and turned, unable to sleep. But the hurt wouldn't go away, it was like a sharp pain that was always there and only time would turn it into a numb ache that would make life bearable again.

She was still awake when she heard Penny go to bed, and later still when she heard footsteps in the lane outside. Her ears pricked and she lay tense, wondering if it was Gyles taking a late night stroll. The footsteps came nearer, slow, unhurried. They paused alongside the house and Kirsty could almost see Gyles in her mind. Was he looking up at her window? Wondering about her? Or was he just wishing that she would get the hell out of his life? After a couple of minutes the footsteps could be heard going back up the lane, moving more briskly now. Kirsty turned her face into the pillow and quietly cried herself to sleep.

She was in a fog, a dense dry fog that threatened to envelop her. And she was hot, so hot. She tried to struggle through the fog, fighting against it because she knew it was vitally urgent that she got through it. But it was so thick that it wrapped itself round her and began to strangle her.

Then, suddenly, she was awake, coughing and gasping for breath. Her eyes were sore and smarting, but she was able to see that the room was full of smoke. Dragging herself out of bed, Kirsty managed to stagger to the window and lean out, her choking lungs grab-

bing gratefully at the pure air, her eyes watering painfully. Above her head she could hear a crackling
sound, and when she looked up she saw to her horror
that the thatch above her room was on fire, the flames
feeding greedily on the dry straw. Her immediate
thought was for Penny and she picked up the first
thing that came to hand to cover her mouth and nose
and made a dash back across the room to the door. The
smoke was so thick that at first she couldn't find it
and had to grope along the wall, banging herself
against the furniture, and taking the cloth away from
her face she tried desperately with both hands to find
the door handle. Immediately she started to inhale the
smoke again and she was almost on her knees when her
panic-stricken fingers found the handle at last.

Thankfully she crawled out of the room and managed to pull the door to behind her. For a few agon-
ised moments she lay on the floor, taking in great
gasps of breath, but then her fear for her sister brought
her to her feet and she managed to get to Penny's
room. But there was hardly any smoke here, it all
seemed to be at her end of the house.

'Penny! Wake up!' She tried to speak loudly,
urgently, but her voice only came out as a gasping croak
and she had to shake the younger girl awake. 'Fire.
Got to get out,' she managed as soon as Penny opened
her eyes.

Somehow they got down the stairs and out of the
back door before Kirsty's legs gave under her and she
collapsed on to the grass while Penny went running to
Mrs Anderson's to phone for the fire brigade, but
when she came back she said someone had already
called them and they were on their way. Everything
seemed to happen at once then. Other neighbours came
rushing along in various stages of dress, some in

dressing-gowns, others with trousers and jackets pulled over their pyjamas. Dave was one of the first to arrive and, after making sure that they were all right, dashed into the house and with several other people started to bring out their furniture and stack it in the garden, while two men with pitchforks tried to pull the burning thatch from the roof.

Kirsty just stood under a tree and watched numbly, unconscious of the chill night air that crept through her thin cotton nightdress and bare feet. The fire was all on the side of the house nearest her bedroom, where the thatch dipped down almost to the hedge. There was a lot of noise and shouting going on around her and several people came up to ask if she was all right, but Kirsty didn't answer them, she didn't even hear them, she could only stare at the fire, her breath still rasping and painful in her throat. And then suddenly Gyles was there. He was dressed but looked as if he had thrown his clothes on in a hurry, his shirt open to the waist, his hair dishevelled. He looked wildly round and then caught hold of the arm of a man who was hurrying past carrying a chair and spoke to him urgently. The man turned to point in her direction, but he'd hardly finished speaking before Gyles was beside her.

'You're safe! Thank God you're safe!' And then she was in his arms and being held so tightly that he hurt her.

But she didn't mind. She had seen the look of overwhelming relief on his face when he'd known that she was safe and nothing else mattered but that. She clung to him unashamedly, oblivious of the people around them, and when he sought her lips she returned his kiss with love and thankfulness, holding nothing back. After he'd raised his head he still held her close, letting her feel the warmth and reassurance of his arms. And it felt so safe, so *right*. A great surge of love and longing ran through her and she trembled with emotion, her face pressed against his shoulder.

Gyles loosened his hold and went to move away, but she immediately pressed close to him again. 'No, don't leave me. Please don't leave me.'

His hand moved to stroke her hair gently as he said softly, 'Only to find you a coat. You're shivering with cold.'

Clutching at his sleeve, Kirsty looked up at him, her eyes misty in her pale face. 'No, I'm not cold. It wasn't that.'

His hands dropped to her shoulders and gripped hard. 'Kirsty.' As he said her name a look of mingled wonder and triumph came into his eyes, and then he said rather ruefully, 'This is a hell of a time to....' But his words were drowned in the wail of the fire engine as it screeched to a stop in the road.

'I'll get you something to put on.' He grinned at her. 'If the firemen see you in just that nightdress they might forget they came to put out the fire!'

He went away and for the first time Kirsty realised just how little she had on, and felt herself blushing when she remembered how close he had held her. But when Gyles came back with her yellow raincoat he helped her into it and belted it up quite matter-of-factly, then produced a pair of Penny's sandals for her to wear.

'They're all I could find, I'm afraid, but at least they'll keep you a little warmer,' he said as he knelt to put them on her.

She put a hand lightly on his shoulder to balance herself and he raised his head to look at her. He didn't speak, but a current of something far more powerful than electricity flowed between them and the look in his eyes told her everything she had longed to hear.

Slowly Gyles got to his feet, his eyes never leaving hers, and it was only when somebody called her name that she reluctantly dragged her eyes away from his face. Turning, she found that Penny was talking to one of the firemen and beckoning her to join them. Gyles took her hand and led her across. Only then did she notice that the fire was out and that the fire crew were making sure that there were no lingering embers.

The fire chief greeted her. 'Miss Naylor, your sister here tells me that you discovered the fire?'

Her voice still rather hoarse, she said, 'Yes, that's right. I woke up and found my room full of smoke.' Involuntarily she shuddered at the memory and Gyles' hand tightened on hers.

'That's the room on the right, nearest the lane?'

'Yes.'

'Have you any idea what caused it, miss?'

Kirsty shook her head. 'No. I wasn't feeling very well and went to bed early.' It seemed so long ago. Then she had been bitterly unhappy because of their quarrel, whereas now—she glanced fleetingly up at Gyles and was immediately reassured—now everything was going to be all right, of that there could be no doubt.

But the fireman was speaking again. 'Were there any flames in your room?'

'No, just smoke. It wasn't until I leaned out of the window to get some air that I saw the flames on the roof.'

'Is there anything else you need to know tonight?' Gyles broke in. 'I really think Miss Naylor ought to see a doctor.'

Kirsty started to protest, but the fire chief said immediately, 'I was going to suggest it myself, Mr Grantham. I expect we'll be able to have a better look in the morning to see what caused the fire.'

He went to turn away, but Gyles gave a sudden exclamation and he turned back and looked at him enquiringly.

'Of course, that must be it! Kirsty, you had a bonfire in the garden earlier. A spark must have carried to the thatch.'

'But I watched it carefully,' she protested. 'And besides, there wasn't any breeze and it was hours ago.'

'Oh, it often doesn't take more than a breath of wind, and the spark could have smouldered in the thatch for some time before it actually took fire,' the fireman told her. 'No, that'll be the cause of it, I reckon. We don't have to look any further.'

Kirsty would have like to argue with him, but talking had irritated her throat and she burst into a fit of coughing.

Gyles looked at her grimly and said to Penny, 'I'm taking you both back to the Manor for the rest of the night. Kirsty must see a doctor at once. Come along, my car's outside.'

He spoke so authoritatively that neither of them thought to disobey him, not that Kirsty wanted to, she was more than happy to place herself in his hands and have him take care of her. But first Penny ran across to tell Dave and he followed them to the car, saying, 'Don't worry about your things. I'll make sure everything's all right here.'

Arriving at the Manor, the girls were taken in hand by an efficient woman who introduced herself as Mrs Grantham's nurse and who led them to a guest suite where she ran baths for them and found clean nightclothes. A doctor arrived soon afterwards and pronounced Penny perfectly all right, but warned Kirsty that her lungs and throat would probably feel sore for a few days.

'But otherwise you're fine, young lady. You had a narrow escape. If you'd swallowed much more smoke you'd have been asphyxiated.'

But even that thought couldn't sober Kirsty's spirits for very long; she was too thankful to be alive—to be alive and in love. She lay quietly in the single bed alongside Penny's and longed for morning to come. Because in the morning she would see Gyles, and she knew that he would make an opportunity for them to be alone together so that he could put into words all the things that his eyes had told her tonight. Her mind filled with the most wonderful thoughts about the future, a dream she still hardly dared to believe might become reality, and she fell asleep with a smile on her lips, still dreaming about tomorrow.

Gyles had given strict orders that they weren't to be disturbed and they slept late; it was after ten before Penny's voice calling her name finally woke her. Kirsty turned lazily, but one look at the unfamiliar surroundings brought her fully awake.

'Look, someone's brought us some clothes,' Penny remarked as she pointed to two of their own suitcases placed just inside the door. 'Dave must have brought them for us.'

'Or Gyles,' Kirsty put in.

Her sister turned to her with a frown as she knelt to undo the cases. 'Come to think of it, you were getting pretty thick with him last night, not to mention letting him bring us back here. You're not falling for him, are you?'

Kirsty gave the ghost of a smile; falling was hardly the word she would have used to describe the almost unbearable feeling of exhilaration and longing that filled her heart. 'Yes, I'm rather afraid I am,' she admitted.

Penny stared at her in horror. 'But Kirsty, you can't! Think of all the things he's done to us.'

Kirsty jumped out of bed and sorted out some clothes to wear. Impatiently she said, 'That wasn't Gyles. I've never really believed that it was and now I'm sure. He just wouldn't do anything like that.' She found some underclothes and chose a pale lavender shirt blouse and a pleated skirt in a darker shade. Thank goodness they'd been in the wardrobe and hadn't been soiled by smoke.

Penny started to argue with her, but Kirsty said earnestly, 'I know I'm right about this.' Then more gently, 'Please, Penny, don't spoil today for me.' And her sister fell silent, although the frown between her brows had deepened.

Gyles wasn't about when they came downstairs, but after they'd eaten a belated breakfast he came to drive them to the cottage. The warmth in his eyes when he greeted her made Kirsty flush a little, but she answered him calmly enough, only her eyes betraying her inner emotions.

When they got to the cottage they found the firemen had arrived there again and were about to fix a tarpaulin over the roof. The chief officer came up to them at once.

'The tarpaulin should keep the weather out for you. Luckily the roof beams weren't too badly damaged and haven't collapsed, although quite a few of them at that end of the house will have to be replaced. The worst mess came from the polythene sheeting that was lining the roof, and it was the fumes from that that made so much smoke. But the house itself isn't damaged much, you should be able to move back in as soon

as we get the tarpaulin up and you've cleaned up a
bit. But you can thank Mr Grantham here for that.
We got here before the fire had spread too much,
thanks to him calling us so promptly.'

Turning to Gyles in surprise, Kirsty said, '*You* called
the fire brigade?'

He nodded. 'I saw the flames from the house.' Then,
glancing at his watch, he added, 'I'm sorry, but I'm
afraid I have to leave you for a while. I have an
appointment in town that I just can't skip, but I'll be
back later this evening.' He drew Kirsty to one side and
put his hands on her upper arms. 'Will you have
dinner with me?'

'Yes, of course.'

His grip tightened slightly and an intense look came
into his grey eyes. 'I want to kiss you.'

She smiled up at him, eyes misty, and raised her
fingers to gently touch his lips. 'I know.' She felt him
quiver and then he quickly caught her hand and buried
a kiss in her palm before he stood back abruptly. For
a moment longer he gazed at her, then he turned and
walked briskly away.

Kirsty didn't come down to earth for quite some
time. Even when they'd changed into old clothes and
begun to remove the effects of the smoke and grime
from the cottage she was still in her own private and
very wonderful world. A world that fell apart an hour
later when the fire chief sought her out, a serious frown
between his brows.

'It seems you were right, Miss Naylor,' he said grimly.
'It wasn't a spark from your bonfire that caused the
fire after all.' He held out a matchbox to her and
Kirsty took it wonderingly. 'We found this on the edge
of the thatch nearest to the lane. Some idiot must have

just flipped it over the hedge, not realising that the roof was so near.'

As Kirsty pushed open the matchbox she suddenly grew very still. She knew that the man was still talking to her, but nothing penetrated. Inside the box there was a cigarette-end. It was black with a thin gold band at the edge of the filter tip. She remembered the sound of Gyles' footsteps halting in the lane outside her window the previous evening. Slowly she became aware that the officer had asked her a question and was waiting for an answer.

'I'm sorry. What—what did you say?'

'I was just saying that it's a very unusual brand of cigarette. I've never seen any like them before. Do you know anyone who smokes them?'

She pushed the matchbox shut. 'No. No, I don't.'

'Well, whoever it was deserves to be shot. You and your sister could easily have been killed.'

He went on further, but Kirsty didn't hear him and presently he and the rest of the firemen left. Numbly Kirsty turned and went into the kitchen, reaching up high to the shelf above the range and putting the matchbox on it, out of sight. Then she slumped down in a chair and gazed blankly into space, the words 'you and your sister could have been killed' going round and round in her head. But when Penny came into the room her voice was quite steady.

'Do you think you could ask Dave to lend you his van so that you can go back to the Manor and collect our cases? And will you see Mrs Grantham and thank her for her hospitality, but say that the cottage is quite habitable so we won't have to bother them again.'

Penny raised her eyebrows in surprise. 'Yes, all right, but don't you want to go yourself?'

'No, I'll stay here and start moving our things back in.' Carefully she turned away so that Penny couldn't see her face. 'And will you ask Mrs Grantham to tell Gyles that I don't feel up to going out tonight?'

Penny's voice rose in concern. 'You're not feeling well? What is it, the smoke?'

Kirsty managed a rather wooden smile. 'No, silly. I went to bed early yesterday because I felt a bit down. It must be the same thing.'

'Then for heaven's sake don't starting lifting the furniture about. Dave can help me to do that this evening. It won't hurt to leave it out there for a bit longer.' Penny came over and looked at her anxiously. 'You look awfully pale. Promise me you'll rest till I get back?'

Kirsty reached out and gripped the younger girl's hand tightly, her eyes dark in her pallid face.

'Kirsty, what is it?' Penny stared at her in alarm.

'Nothing. Just—shock, I suppose.' She gave a tight smile. 'Hurry back.'

For the rest of the day she behaved more like a robot than a human being. She moved and walked and talked, but it was as if the part of her that had thoughts and feelings had been shut away in a cupboard because the reality was too unbearable even to contemplate. In the evening Dave came round and helped them with the furniture and stayed to supper. He reminded them that they should inform the insurance company straight away, so Kirsty sat down and wrote a letter. She was glad to do it, to do anything that would put off the moment when she would have to face the bitterness of her own thoughts.

'Did the firemen find out definitely what caused the fire?' Dave asked them.

'They think it must have been a spark from the bonfire, don't they, Kirsty?' Penny answered.

Kirsty hesitated for only a second before saying firmly, 'Yes, that's what they said.'

It was nearly dusk by the time she had finished her letter and she decided to go and post it at once. Light rain had fallen earlier and there were still some clouds helping to darken the sky, so she put on her coat and walked slowly along to the village post office which had a letter box built into the wall. Afterwards she went to sit on the wooden bench on the green for a while so that Dave and Penny could have some time alone together. She tried not to let herself think about the past but only about the future, and of that there could no longer be any doubt. They must put Briar Cottage up for sale at once. Whether they left the district completely didn't matter, but she didn't dare take the risk of anything else happening to them. It was obvious that their enemy would stop at nothing now to get rid of them; it had gone far beyond attempts to ruin them financially, now their very lives had been placed in danger. And she must, for Penny's sake as well as her own, let their assailant know that he had won by putting the house up for sale as soon as possible. That way they would probably be safe from any future attacks until they left.

Even now when everything seemed to point to Gyles, Kirsty still could hardly admit to herself that he was guilty. Only last night she had been convinced that he returned her feelings, that he loved her and had been on the point of telling her so. It was just impossible for someone to have deliberately tried to set the house on fire and then behaved towards her as he had. They'd have to be mad to do.... That thought froze her mind for several minutes until she remembered that it was Gyles who called the fire brigade. Why would he have

done that if he'd wanted to harm them? Because he
didn't want the house to burn down, because he only
wanted to scare them. Against her will the answers
came unbidden into her mind. Her thoughts raged
back and forth, her reason accusing and her heart de-
fending, until she felt as if she was going mad herself,
and she was still no nearer to a solution. She longed to
trust him, but for Penny's sake she knew she dared not
take the risk.

It was quite dark when she rose and began to walk
back towards the cottage, and the old-fashioned lamps
dotted at intervals round the green were already lit,
attracting moths to their bulbs. As she walked she tried
to decide how she could best persuade Penny to leave
without having to tell her about the cigarette-end, for
she was determined to keep that to herself. The noise
of a car engine made her look up and she recognised
Gyles' white Range-Rover as it passed under a lamp
further down the road, travelling towards her. Her
pulse began to beat faster as she wondered whether he
would stop and speak to her, if he had come to look
for her even. What could she say to him? How could
she face him? Her footsteps slowed and she waited
tremblingly at the side of the road, clearly visible in
the lamplight. Dimly she could make out the figure
of a man in the driver's seat. He must have recognised
her by now, but he didn't appear to be slowing down,
if anything he was going faster. Kirsty stood transfixed
in the roadway, unable to move as the Range-Rover
sped towards her and she realised it was coming
straight at her, its headlights blazing. For several petri-
fying moments she was too stunned to accept what her
senses were telling her and it was only at the last in-
stant that a subconscious sense of self-preservation

brought life back to her limbs and she leapt out of the way.

But those few paralysed seconds had cost Kirsty dear, for even as she thought she was safe, the skirt of her coat caught on the back bumper of the vehicle and she was thrown to the ground and dragged helplessly along like a rag doll. Flinging up her arms, she managed to cover her face, but she was pulled along for several yards before the material gave and she was left lying in a huddled heap on the ground.

From somewhere a long way off she could hear some-one crying, great choking sobs of terror and hurt, and it was some time before she realised that it was her own voice. She didn't know how she got to her feet or why she didn't call for help, she remembered nothing until she staggered into the kitchen of Briar Cottage and fell on the floor. Looking up into the appalled faces of Dave and Penny, she said in a dead, empty voice, 'He tried to kill me. Gyles tried to kill me.' She would have given anything to have passed out then, to have sunk into a blessed oblivion that shut out all memory and all feelings, but even that was denied her; she was fully conscious, fully aware that the man she loved had deliberately tried to run her down.

Dave was talking to her, asking questions, his voice sharp and urgent, while Penny, her face almost as white as her own, had brought a basin and was starting to bathe her hands. It was almost with surprise that Kirsty saw that they were bleeding, the backs of them badly grazed; she could feel no pain, only this great torment of anguish in her heart.

'Kirsty!' Dave was almost shouting at her in his urgency and she slowly raised her head to look at him, her eyes dark with numb despair. 'Kirsty, you must try to tell me what happened. Do you understand?'

She nodded and answered dully, 'I told you; he tried to kill me.'

'Gyles Grantham?'

'Yes. He drove his Range-Rover at me. I jumped out of the way but my coat got caught and I got dragged along for a little way. Look.' To convince them she turned on the chair they'd lifted her into and showed them the great rent in her coat. 'Look,' she said again, rather like a child who is afraid of not being believed.

'But Kirsty, it must have been an accident. The Squire wouldn't run you down on purpose.' Dave's voice was incredulous, disbelieving.

'Oh, wouldn't he?' It was Penny's furious voice that answered. 'You don't know the half of it.' She started to pour into Dave's ears the details of everything that had happened to them since they came to Notley. Kirsty made a futile attempt to stop her but then subsided into the chair, her face bleak and hopeless.

'But most of that is purely circumstantial,' Dave said when she'd finished. 'You have no proof that it was the Squire.'

'I know, that's why Kirsty wouldn't let me go to the police.' Penny turned to her. 'But you say it was him who knocked you down. Are you sure, Kirsty, really sure?'

'Oh, yes, I'm sure.' Her voice flat, almost emotionless, she went on, 'I made him angry, you see, terribly angry. He forbade me to help his mother, but I went ahead anyway. He said that he could kill me for what I'd done, but I didn't think he meant it.' Her voice began to shake and she laughed, a strange, unnatural sound. 'How stupid can you get? A man tells you he wants to kill you and you don't believe him.' She gazed at their horrified faces unseeingly, her mouth twisted in irony. 'Even when I knew he'd set fire to the thatch I still wouldn't let myself believe that it was him. It wasn't until I saw his car driving at me that I ... that I....' She began to shake violently, the fear coming back and engulfing her again.

'Kirsty, it's all right now. You're safe. Safe with us.' Penny put her arms round her and cradled her like a child.

She heard their voices above her head and then Penny was holding a glass to her mouth and ordering her to drink its contents. Gradually the shaking eased and the dull numbness took over once more.

Dave was on his knees beside her, looking at her earnestly. 'Try and concentrate just a little longer, Kirsty. You said that Gyles Grantham set light to the thatch, but you told Penny and me it was a spark from the bonfire. What made you change your mind?'

Painfully she replied in a low voice, 'I lied to you. I didn't want to frighten Penny. I thought that if we put the house up for sale and went away....' She broke off and nodded towards the fireplace. 'On the shelf over the range you'll find a matchbox with a cigarette-end in it. The firemen found it this morning in the thatch near the lane and gave it to me. It's a brand that only Gyles smokes, he orders them specially from abroad. I suppose he thought it would be consumed in the fire.'

Before she'd finished speaking Dave had hurried to find the matchbox and open it. His face was grim as he said, 'Yes, I remember noticing that he smoked some like this at your party. That settles it, then. With this evidence the police will be able to pick him up at once.'

'The police?' Kirsty had been slumped in her chair but now she pushed herself up. 'No, you can't go to the police. We'll just leave here, go away tonight. We'll go to London. It doesn't matter where we go as long as we leave here. He won't come after us, he only wants us to go away.' She began to babble incoherently, her numb brain unable to cope with the need to find words to convince him.

But Dave rounded on her, his voice angry. 'Are you crazy? He cold-bloodedly tried to run you down and for all he knew left you lying dead in the road! And you could both have been burnt to death in your beds last night! Not only you, Kirsty, but Penny as well,' he said forcefully. 'And if you think I'm going to stand by and let anyone—even the Squire—get away with that, then you underestimate me.' His voice softened as he saw the stricken look on her face. 'I know you're frightened out of your wits, but once the police have been told and they've taken him into custody, you will be quite safe from him, you won't have to be afraid any more.'

It was Penny who said in a hollow voice, 'Kirsty isn't afraid *of* him, she's afraid *for* him. She's in love with him.'

Dave stared at them both in dumbfounded silence, then he said sadly, 'Oh, my God! You poor kid.' He shook his head. 'I'm sorry, Kirsty, but it's got to be done. You must see that.' He tried to take her hands but quickly let them go again when she flinched with pain.

Slowly she nodded. 'All right. I suppose I've known all along there's no other way.' Leaning back in the chair, she closed her eyes, too exhausted to go on fighting any more.

Events then seemed to be like snatches from a film; some stood out clearly in her mind, others she was hardly aware of. She supposed that Dave went out to send for the police, but she didn't see him go, only realising that they had actually arrived when a middle-aged man with iron-grey hair and alert eyes behind

his world-weary expression began to question her all
over again. She answered him as honestly as she could,
but her voice often trailed away into a miserable
silence until he brought her back with a gentle re-
minder. It was Penny's turn then and she replied far
more vehemently, her voice angry and bitter. Some
time, Kirsty wasn't sure when exactly, Dr King came
to examine her and when she took off her jeans she
found that she was badly grazed all down one leg, from
her hip to her knee, where she'd been dragged along
the ground. He cleaned her up, gave her an anti-
tetanus injection, bandaged her hands, and gave her
some tablets to kill the pain. Kirsty took them reluctantly; she would have been glad of a physical pain to
replace the numb emptiness she was feeling now. The
doctor wanted her to go to bed, but she steadfastly refused, putting on clean clothes and going to sit quietly
downstairs again, watching, waiting, her nerves as
tense as bowstrings.

Most of the policemen went away, but some time
later the Inspector came back again and said that she
would have to go to the police station in Barham to
make a statement. She went without a word. Penny
sat beside her in the car and tried to comfort her, but
she hardly knew that her sister was even there. At the
station they asked her everything all over again while
someone took it down, and then she had to read
through what she'd said and sign her name. After that
nothing happened for quite a while and she just sat
in a chair feeling utterly weary and dejected. But she
didn't want to go home and go to bed. Because if she
fell asleep she might dream, and she knew with utmost
certainty the terrible form the dream would take.

Voices sounded suddenly in the corridor outside,
loud and angry. She recognised Gyles' voice as it cut

through the others, harsh and demanding. Slowly, her nerves at screaming point, she rose to her feet. Dave and Penny, their tones alarmed, were talking urgently across her, but she didn't hear them. Without warning the door burst open and Gyles stood on the threshold, his eyes blazing savagely in his taut face. One glance found her and he took a hasty step into the room. Dave immediately moved to protect her from him just as two uniformed constables dashed into the room after Gyles and caught his arms. For a moment he resisted them, then he shrugged and bit out, 'All right, I'm coming, damn you!' His eyes locked with hers, burning into her brain, shrivelling her up inside, and then he was gone, striding abruptly away.

Kirsty sank slowly back into her chair, her eyes staring at the empty doorway. She had known it would be hard, but never as bad as this; she felt as if something had died inside her, something that she would grieve and sorrow over for the rest of her life.

Vaguely she heard Dave saying, 'Now that they've got him, I'm going to find out if we can leave. You both look fagged to death.'

'No,' Kirsty broke in immediately. 'You must take Penny home, but I'm going to stay here until—until I know what they're going to do with him.'

'But, Kirsty love, there's nothing you can do now. Please come back to the cottage and get some sleep,' Penny implored her.

Kirsty's eyes were dark with unhappiness as she turned to her sister. 'I can't. Please try to understand. I—I just have to stay here until I know for sure.'

'Then we'll all stay,' Dave said resignedly.

So the waiting began again. A friendly policewoman brought them cups of tea and then Dave dozed in his chair while Penny fell asleep with her head on his shoulder, but Kirsty was wide awake, alert to any sound that might give her some news of Gyles. And presently she heard people moving in the corridor and looked out in time to see Gyles and the Inspector and a couple of policemen get into a police car and drive away. But her anxious question put to the constable on duty at the desk only elicited the information that 'they were pursuing their enquiries'.

Kirsty was immediately tortured by all sorts of mental pictures, imagining him being taken away to a prison, being locked up in a cell. Why wouldn't someone come and tell her what was happening? She dug her nails into her palms as hard as she could. This waiting was unbearable. It was half an hour before she heard anything more, and then when she opened the door she found her view blocked by the back of a burly policeman and she only caught a glimpse of the back of Gyles' head as he walked down the corridor with several other men. Shortly afterwards Dave and Penny woke up as the Inspector came into the room and sat down in the chair across the table from them.

Kirsty gazed at him anxiously and said in little more than a whisper, 'What—what are you going to do with him?'

The man looked at her from under his shaggy eyebrows and filled his pipe before replying. 'With Mr Grantham? Nothing, he's free to go.' They all stared at him in amazement and he went on, 'You see, Mr Grantham was able to prove that he'd been at home at the time you were being run down, and his Range-Rover locked up in the garage. So that meant we had to look for someone else, and here Mr Grantham was able to help us.' He paused while he pulled on his pipe until Kirsty felt like screaming at him to go on. 'He told us that he bought an identical Range-Rover which is used exclusively at the garden centre, for deliveries and that sort of thing. So we went along to the manager, Alan Morris's, house and had a look at that Range-Rover. He said that he hadn't been out in it tonight, but when we examined it we found several threads from your mackintosh still attached to the rear bumper. Then, after—hmm—a little persuasion, the whole story came out. It seems he intended to buy Briar Cottage when it came up for auction, wanted to turn it into a market garden. Mr Grantham had known about this, of course, and his own man had had instructions not to start bidding unless the price went too high for Morris, in which case he would buy the place and rent it to Morris. But you came along and put paid to all that,' he added, nodding at Kirsty and Penny.

'Of course when Morris found out that the Squire wanted to get rid of you and ordered him not to serve you, he was highly delighted, but then Mr Grantham changed his mind and seemed to want you to stay. It was then Morris decided to get rid of you himself and put the blame on the Squire, who, he considered, had let him down. When he saw you cutting your hedge he decided to come back one night and put some yew clippings in the field to poison the Squire's cows. He also let the animals into your garden and put sugar in your petrol tank. But you still stayed on, and he began to get vindictive, especially when he saw you and Mr Grantham together when the Squire called at the garden centre.' The Inspector paused, then said matter-of-factly, 'So he set fire to your thatch.'

'But the cigarette-end?' It was Dave who asked, the two girls were too stunned to speak.

The Inspector shrugged. 'Nothing simpler. Mr Grantham smoked a cigarette while he was in Morris's office and stubbed it out in his ashtray. Morris merely relit it and tossed it on the roof. He says that he didn't intend to do you any harm, simply to frighten you off.'

'But it was Gyles Grantham who drove at her. Kirsty saw him.'

The Inspector shook his head. 'She saw a man. She saw a Range-Rover. And her mind put two and two together and came up with the only person she knew who owned a Range-Rover. Natural enough, especially after all the things had happened that pointed at the Squire.' He went on, 'Morris says he did it on impulse. He saw Miss Naylor walking along the road and drove the vehicle towards her to scare her, make her jump out of the way.' He looked at Kirsty enquiringly. 'But he says you didn't jump—you just stood there waiting for him to come at you until the last second. That you had plenty of time to get out of the way.'

'I—I couldn't move. I thought—I thought it was Gyles.'

'You didn't see the driver clearly?'

Slowly she shook her head. 'The headlights were blazing into my eyes. I saw a man—and I was so sure it was him.' She looked at the Inspector, her face stricken. 'I'm so terribly sorry.'

He shrugged. 'As I said, a natural mistake.' He looked at her not unkindly. 'But you should have come to me with your suspicions before, young lady. It would have saved a lot of unpleasantness, not to mention the damage to your property.' He rose to his feet. 'And now I suggest you all go home and get some sleep for what's left of the night. I'll let you know when we'll need you to give evidence at Morris's trial.'

He went to leave, but Kirsty said quickly, 'Please. Mr

Grantham—where is he?'

The Inspector's face set into disapproving lines. 'He's here. Having a few grazes plastered, I shouldn't wonder. When Morris realised that the game was up he made a run for it, and Grantham, very incorrectly, pushed my men out of the way and went after him himself. There was a rather nasty little free-for-all before we got there and broke it up.'

When he'd gone, Dave and Penny immediately began to exclaim over the Inspector's story, marvelling that Morris could have been the culprit and no one suspect him. They tried to ask her opinion, but Kirsty answered only in monosyllables, her mind so overwhelmingly full of relief that she could think of nothing else. Presently Dave helped her to her feet and, almost in a daze, she allowed him to lead her out of the police station. She must have said goodnight to the duty constable, but she hardly remembered doing so, and it wasn't until they were standing on the steps outside and the cold night air hit her that she realised they were taking her home.

'No, I can't go home yet,' she protested as Dave went to draw her towards his car. 'I have to stay and see Gyles.'

'But, Kirsty, you can see him in the morning. You're nearly dropping on your feet as it is, and Penny's not much better.'

Kirsty looked contritely at her sister. 'I'm sorry, I know you're tired.' She tried to pull herself together and said more firmly, 'Look, there's no need for us all to stay. You take Penny home and I'll follow as soon as I can. I'm sure the police will give me a lift.'

Dave started to argue. 'But Kirsty, a few hours aren't going to make any difference.'

Painfully she looked at him and said, 'Dave, tonight

I accused a man of trying to murder me. I can't just walk away without a word. I *have* to see him, to try to apologise to him somehow.'

He studied her face for a moment and then nodded. 'All right. I'll take Penny home now, but if you get stuck phone me at the garage and I'll come straight back and pick you up.'

Her eyes were warm as she looked at him. 'Thanks, Dave. I don't know what we would have done without you tonight. Take care of Penny for me.'

Dave turned to put his arm round the younger girl and looked at her tenderly. 'Oh, I intend to,' he said. 'Permanently.' And he firmly led Penny away, blushing furiously but radiantly happy.

Kirsty watched them go, greatly comforted to know that Penny's future was settled. But of her own she had serious misgivings. Slowly she limped back into the police station, the pain in her grazed leg more acute now she was walking on it. The duty constable wasn't behind the desk and for a moment she hesitated, wondering where to wait. But one look at the wooden, benchlike seat in the corridor made her decide to go back into the room where they'd been sitting; at least there the seats were reasonably comfortable. She flopped down into a chair, her bad leg stretched out in front of her. Fatigue swept over her in waves and she longed to sleep. She must only have had about five hours in the last two days, she realised as she leaned her head back against the wall and closed her eyes. She would rest for just a minute, just until Gyles left.

It was the sound of voices in the corridor that awakened her from the uneasy doze she had fallen into, and for a moment she couldn't think where she was, but one look at the bare cream walls of the room brought her back to her senses and she sat up with a jerk. She recognised Gyles' voice then, he seemed to be enquiring something of the policeman at the desk. Quickly she got to her feet, but almost fell as her leg gave under her. Oh, darn! It had stiffened up while she'd been sitting there. Despairingly she called, 'Gyles!' and hurried into the corridor as fast as she could, her leg dragging behind her.

The constable looked at her in surprise. 'Why, I thought you'd gone with your sister, miss.'

Kirsty didn't answer but half ran to the main door and out into the night. To her left she heard the sound of an engine starting up and then the headlights of Gyles' Range-Rover began to move forward as he drove towards the exit from the car park. For a moment she gazed after him in despair, some deep-down instinct telling her that she had to talk to him, to put things right now, tonight. Without pausing to think about it, she turned to the right and began to run as fast as she could towards the main road of the town. The police station car park, she remembered, turned into a side road and Gyles would have to drive a few hundred yards before he turned into the High Street and headed for Notley. If she could only get there first! She ran on, forcing her leg to work, her breath coming in pain-filled gasps. Past some houses where a dog began to bark at the sound of her steps, then the back of the shops. Dimly she heard the sound of the car engine carrying clearly through the stillness of the night. Oh, please, please let me be in time! Her hopes began to rise as she started down an alley leading to the High Street where sodium lamps shone brightly. Then suddenly something shot across her path. Kirsty automatically swerved to avoid it, but the change of balance to her stiff leg sent her sprawling headlong while the cat spat at her before leaping on to a wall.

With a sob, she dragged herself to her feet and carried on, the sound of the car loud in her ears now. Desperately she ran out of the alley and straight into the middle of the road, putting up her hands in a futile effort to stop him. It was the nightmare all over again; the glaring headlights, the snarl of the engine. Only this time she didn't jump out of the way, she just stood there, waiting.

There was a shriek of brakes as the tires bit into the road, leaving black streaks of rubber on the surface. The engine cut and then the headlights. Slowly Kirsty opened her eyes. The hood of the Range-Rover was less than two yards away. She heard Gyles get out of the car and slowly turned to look at him.

His voice was rough, unsteady. 'You little fool, you could have been killed! Isn't once tonight enough for you?'

'I—I'm sorry. I had to see you, talk to you.'

'Where did you come from?'

'The police station. I was waiting.'

'They told me you'd gone.'

'No, I stayed behind. Gyles, please, I know you're furious with me and that what I did was unforgivable, but I had to try and make you understand.'

'There's no need, the Inspector explained everything,' he replied shortly.

'No, not everything. He didn't know how hard I tried not to suspect you—in my heart I don't think I ever did really, but—but I had Penny to think about. I couldn't take even the slightest chance of anything happening to her.' She paused, but Gyles remained motionless, just watching her. 'How—how do you go about apologising to someone for accusing them of murder?' She shrugged helplessly. 'I can only say that I'm sorry, terribly sorry, but I never really believed it was you. I'm not trying to condone what I did, I know you'll never forgive me, but I had to tell you.' She looked searchingly into his face, but his expression was unreadable, closed-in.

Miserably she said, 'I shouldn't have bothered you with this tonight, you've been through enough. I'll go now.' Turning away, she began to move towards the pavement.

'Where are you going?' His voice sounded sharp.

'Back to the police station. They'll give me a lift back to Notley.'

'Get in the car. I'll take you home.' Then, as she hesitated, 'I said get in the car, Kirsty.'

Slowly she turned and began to limp towards the passenger side. Instantly he was beside her. 'You're hurt? They didn't tell me you'd been hurt. Oh, Kirsty, my darling, my little love, what did that murdering swine do to you?'

His arms came round to hold her and Kirsty's heart began to pound. 'It's nothing really, just grazes where I got dragged along the ground for a bit.' She heard him swear sharply under his breath, but then she moved a little away from him to look pleadingly into his face. 'Oh, Gyles, say you forgive me. Please, please, say you forgive me!'

'Crazy idiot!' His voice was thick as he bent to kiss her. 'I never blamed you. They told me how you tried to protect me. I just blame myself for not having realised what was going on. It was *I* who should have been protecting *you*. I wanted to see you and put things right between us straight away, but they insisted on taking my statement first. Oh, Kirsty, Kirsty, if only I'd known!'

Her arms slid round his neck. 'I wanted to tell you,

to trust you. After the fire I was sure that you—that you cared a little and I....'

'That I loved you, you mean' he said as his arms tightened round her and his eyes looked deep into hers.

A little incoherently she went on, 'I wanted to tell you then, but there was no opportunity, and then—then they showed me the cigarette-end.' Her voice trailed off and she looked away.

'Oh, my poor sweet, what a hell of a mess Morris made for us! If ever I get my hands on him....'

Kirsty laughed unsteadily. 'From what the Inspector said you already have.' She put up a finger and gently touched the plaster covering a cut over his eye. 'Were you badly hurt?'

'Just that cut and a few scraped knuckles. But it was worth, it by God it was. I could have killed him for what he did to you. If I'd known that you'd been injured....'

'Hush!' Kirsty put her fingers over his mouth. 'It's over now. We must forget it ever happened.'

He smiled, his eyes tender, as he kissed her fingers. 'Mm. And besides, we have far more interesting things to think about.' Swinging her up, he carried her to his car and put her in the passenger seat, then climbed in beside her. He looked at her pale face. 'You must be exhausted, I'd better get you home,' he said in concern.

He started to drive out of the town, one hand coming to cover hers as he turned often to smile at her, his dark eyes filled with pride and love.

Kirsty felt tired, yes, but was too full of exhilarating happiness to sleep, and she didn't want this night to end, not yet. So presently she said softly, 'Gyles.'

'Mm?'

'Couldn't you possibly run out of gas?'

His head turned quickly to look at her and then he gave a soft chuckle. 'What a very good idea!' And soon he turned off the road and drew up under some trees. He reached for her then with a kind of hunger and kissed her with a fierceness that took her by surprise. His lips were firm and demanding a response, their pressure increasing until he forced her lips apart. From the moment he took her in his arms he established an absolute mastery over her and unhesitatingly she submitted to a sexual domination she had never imagined could exist. At her response, his kiss became more passionate, more inflamed, and Kirsty moaned at the wave of sensuality he aroused in her.

'Oh, Gyles, I love you so much,' she breathed as his lips left her mouth at last and began to explore her eyes, her cheek, her neck.

At that he lifted his head and looked at her questioningly. 'Your boy-friend? Simon?'

Kirsty flushed. 'There was never anything more between us than a few kisses. That night you saw us together in the bedroom—it wasn't what you think. We didn't. . . .'

Gyles interrupted her swiftly. 'It doesn't matter. I never believed that he was your lover.' He smiled. 'I was just infernally jealous of him, that was all. But I went through hell thinking that you were in love with him and wanted to marry him. Tell me that you don't care for him any more, darling.'

'I don't. I broke with him that night. I—I found that I just didn't want him to touch me any more. It was when I saw you both together that I realised just how my feelings had changed and that I so much wanted you to be. . . .' She faltered and couldn't go on.

'To be the one to hold you in his arms and tell you he loves you?' Gyles finished for her softly.

'Yes. Oh, yes, Please, Gyles!'

And as he drew her towards him he whispered, 'Always and for ever, my dearest.'

It was a long time before he let her go again, but when he did, she said hesitantly, 'Your mother; you were so angry?'

He smiled rather ruefully. 'She let me know in no uncertain terms that you were right about that. She's taking an apartment in London to be near the hospital where she's to undergo the treatment. She has every confidence in it and seems a different woman.' He drew her closer to him. 'I've been wrong about a hell of a lot of things where you're concerned, in fact there's only one thing that I've been sure about all along.'

'Oh, what was that?'

He bent to trace the outline of her neck with his lips. 'That I've been going mad with longing for you almost since the first time I met you, and if you don't hurry up and marry me I won't answer for the consequences.'

Dawn was about to break in the sky before they at last drew up outside Briar Cottage. May blossom hung in the hedges like a bridal veil and its heavy scent filled their nostrils as they got out of the car. Slowly, reluctantly almost, they walked up the garden path and kissed lingeringly in the porch. At last Gyles let her go and turned the key for her.

Kirsty went to go inside but stopped with a sudden exclamation. 'Oh, look! The first of the roses has started to come out.' She pointed and Gyles reached up to pluck it for her. 'Why, it's yellow! So we were both wrong.' She looked up at the rambler that climbed almost to the roof. 'Soon it will be a mass of blooms.'

'Just in time to use them in your wedding bouquet.'

She turned to him, her eyes radiant with happiness.
'That soon?'

'Definitely that soon.' And Gyles drew her to him
as above them the dawn proclaimed its coming with
golden flutes into the clear sky and on the distant
horizon the sun blazed into the heavens to herald the
new day.

Harlequin understands...

the way you feel about love

Harlequin novels are stories of
people in love—people like you—
and all are beautiful romances,
set in exotic faraway places.

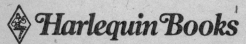

Available at your favorite store or from the
Harlequin Reader Service.

In the U.S.A.:
M.P.O. Box 707
Niagara Falls, N.Y. 14302

In Canada:
649 Ontario Street
Stratford, Ontario N5A 6W2

And there's still *more* love in

Yes!

Six more spellbinding
romantic stories every month
by your favorite authors.
Elegant and sophisticated tales of
love and love's conflicts.

Let your imagination be swept away to
exotic places in search of adventure,
intrigue and romance. Get to
know the warm, true-to-life
characters. Share the special
kind of miracle that
love can be.

Don't miss out. Buy now and discover
the world of HARLEQUIN PRESENTS...

Harlequin Romances

The books that let you escape
into the wonderful world of romance!
Trips to exotic places... interesting
plots... meeting memorable people...
the excitement of love.... These are
integral parts of Harlequin Romances —
the heartwarming novels read by
women everywhere.

Many early issues are now available.
Choose from this great selection!

Choose from this list of Harlequin Romance editions.*

*Some of these book were originally published under different titles